HERESIES

Heresies

Resist Much, Obey Little

Ken Coates

United States distributor
DUFOUR EDITIONS, INC.
Booksellers and Publishers
Chester Springs, PA 19425
215-458-5005

Spokesman

Free state — what is this?

It is by no means the aim of the workers, who have got rid of the narrow mentality of humble subjects, to set the state free . . . Freedom consists in converting the state from an organ superimposed upon society into one completely subordinate to it . . .

Karl Marx: *The Critique of the Gotha Programme*

To the States or any one of them, or any city of the States, *Resist much, obey little*,
Once unquestioning obedience, once fully enslaved,
Once fully enslaved, no nation, state, city of this earth,
ever afterward resumes its liberty.

Walt Whitman: To the States, *Leaves of Grass*

First published in Great Britain in 1982 by Spokesman
Bertrand Russell House, Gamble Street, Nottingham NG7 4ET

Coates, Ken
Heresies.
1. Communism — History — 20th century
I. Title
335.43'09 HX40

ISBN 0-85124-355-X
ISBN 0-85124-356-8 Pbk

Printed by the Russell Press Ltd., Nottingham

Contents

Introduction

In 1955, Bertrand Russell and Albert Einstein published the famous manifesto which launched the Pugwash movement, so named because the first international meeting of scientists which it called into being met at Cyrus Eaton's estate in Pugwash, Canada.

This document set out the classic statement of the perils of nuclear war, which, its authors established, might quite possibly put an end to the human race. Their judgement has lost none of its validity. But the political disputes which divide the world have changed significantly since Russell and Einstein agreed their text. "The world is full of conflicts", they wrote, "and, overshadowing all minor conflicts, the titanic struggle between communism and anti-communism". Two and a half decades on, this "titanic struggle" has radically changed its form.

Even in 1955, anti-communism had many exponents, from quasi-feudal despots, to the directors of great capitalist corporations, to social democrats or libertarian socialists. Those opposing communism in 1980 represent a no less incompatible spectrum than before, although the shades of opinion included in it are now perhaps more finely delineated. On the other side, those supporting communism have fragmented into a dizzying variety of schools. There are Soviet communists, and Chinese communists; Albanians and Yugoslavs; Cubans and Euro-communists. Doctrinal disagreements follow these national and regional cleavages, and also, to some degree, overlay them. In capitalist countries, there are in the 1980s a kaleidoscope of small, and not so small, groupings reflecting and further fracturing these arguments. There are Trotskyists and Maoists, followers of Stalin and innumerable socialists who wish to find their way back to Marx.

Between actual states, these arguments have not remained

9

verbal. Military exchanges have taken place between the USSR and China across a heavily armed frontier. A whole network of nuclear shelters was subsequently constructed in Chinese cities as a defence against possible Soviet attack. Soviet SS-20s ring China, just as they are also targetted upon Europe. Armies of the Warsaw Pact have intervened in force to change the policies and depose the Government of Czechoslovakia. Vietnam has invaded Cambodia, and established a puppet government to replace the communists of the Khmers Rouges, who are now accused in a worldwide public relations campaign of being as bad as, if not worse than, the Nazis. China has invaded Vietnam and exacted heavy losses of life and materials in order to administer what her leaders have described as a "lesson". It is unfortunately not entirely excluded that a second such "lesson" may follow. Following the example and teaching of Stalin in the Soviet Union, communist revolutions in China, Indochina, and elsewhere have been integrally interwoven with nationalism, and while this powerful influence has at times increased their appeal to their domestic populations, it has also corroded the alleged internationalism of communism, producing in the end a variety of more or less overtly antagonistic "communisms".

Not a whit less divided is the capitalist world. Whilst multinational companies establish a new globalism, serious divisions of economic interest separate the United States from the most potent European nations, and there are widening breaches between both of these power centres and their dynamic competitors in Japan. If conventional socialist doctrines on imperialism are true, then the real world conflict is as likely to follow inter-capitalist fractures as it is to remain contained in the ideological rupture of the cold war. At the same time realistic "western" analysis can show that ideological quarrels have relatively easily become exchanges of shot and shell between "communist" states, whilst the basic East-West divide has remained frozen in an uneasy peace.

In the developing confrontation between the two great super-powers which followed the Soviet invasion of Afghanistan, not only did many of the major communist parties declare themselves neutral to a greater or lesser extent, but one of the more significant dimensions of growing tension emerged in the increasingly apparent, if probably impermanent, alignment of American and Chinese interests. On the other side, fierce disputes are carried on behind closed doors as different European states contest the United States' attempts to impede the construction of a gas pipeline from the USSR.

All this has made the maintenance of peace immeasurably more difficult, since the complex of shifting affinities involves risk that where one dispute between two contenders might be negotiated to a settlement, the actions of a third party may serve to reopen old divisions on a new plane, or create new conflicts immediately after the resolution of existing ones. That more than one of the potential contenders phrase their communiques in the language of Marxism, with quotations from the same scriptures, by no means ameliorates this difficulty.

The fragmentation of interests within the blocs makes the old concept of detente infinitely more difficult to pursue. Even if all the statesmen in all the powers were firmly bent on avoiding war at all costs, they would require consummate expertise and skill to do so. However, it seems rather plain that peace is not exactly the first priority for all of them, so that the avoidance of war requires other advocates, with firmer commitments, if it is to be adequately promoted.

All this would have been a warning to heed even if each of the worlds of Russell and Einstein had simply subdivided: but in fact both parts of their world have also entered other profound crises. Fission has followed crisis, and aggravated it in the process. Apparent economic stability in the West has given way to deep slump, mass unemployment, and aggravated civil disorder in many countries. The once monolithic political conformity of the East has also broken into serial problems, promoting apathy, withdrawal and even non-co-operation on a wide scale. Strident dissidence has become evident among certain minorities. In both halves of this cold peace, troubles now come, not in single spies, but in whole battalions.

However complex the evolution of affairs since they wrote their manifesto, Russell and Einstein were right to pinpoint what has remained the unresolved problem of our time, to which we may find no simple solution in any scriptures, secular or other. In a prophetic moment more than a hundred years earlier, the authors of the Communist Manifesto had spoken of the class struggle (which they clearly saw as a democratic process in the fullest sense of the words), as ending "either in a revolutionary reconstitution of society at large or in the common ruin of the contending classes.''

That "common ruin" now looms over us. It is no longer a question of socialism or barbarism, but of survival or the end of our species. Although this dilemma has confronted us since the Hiroshima explosion in August 1945, we have neither adequately understood it, nor have we yet resolved it.

Yet the existence of this dilemma does not at all annul the other lesser social tensions which demand real change in the structures of our societies, East and West alike.

As is made clear in the chapters which follow, it is my passionate belief that there could be a socialism which based itself on the continuous development and expansion of democracy, including and upholding every freedom of expression and association. This development of democratic accountability throughout the political and economic processes seems to me to be more, not less, relevant in an age where authority is concentrated to beyond hitherto dreamable strengths. The bomb itself is the ultimate achievement of arbitrary power. Dr Strangelove is the last, most dreadful usurper. Only by rendering all the acts of Government transparent and all the deeds of power answerable to those over whom it is exercised can we reach any short term hope of continuing human evolution, even into the next century.

It does not help the achievement of such hopes to prettify the tensions which ravage this modern world. This book looks only at some of the issues, which have made themselves apparent in the tortured evolution of those states which describe themselves as socialist, and those parties in Western Europe which call themselves communist.

The socialists and independent communists in Western Europe have a special responsibility to grasp and act upon these global disorders. They are still free enough to see straight, and organised enough to set an example.

Of course, a lot of words and a lot of blood have combined over the years to separate socialist and communist traditions in Europe. Yet there remains an uneasy sense of common origins, and perhaps a hesitant fraternity, not completely forgotten even while all the horrors of a dreadful century are strongly remembered.

Two world wars already, and a third and culminating firestorm in preparation, have laid claim to enough dead, without counting the uncountable victims of other pitiless social struggles. It is clear that such struggles have continued and widened throughout our epoch in spite of the increasing danger that they might spill out of control to embroil others far beyond their immediate reach. Little wars are always with us. Also with us always is the prospect that each or any of them could roll away to become big.

Within this nightmare reality, all the brave and simple political ideals have been stalemated or nullified. Socialism has been sundered from democracy, stifling both in the process. Communism as a state system has been overcome by often rabid chauvinism, suffocating its universal promise. It has been contact with imperial capitalism which has rescued the Chinese revolution from the excesses of involution and xenophobia, at a cost not yet to be calculated. Detente may yet prove to have helped the evolution of socialism, however.

If it matters, Karl Marx is turning in his grave as most of this news filters down to him. It has been dripping through for a long time.

It is perfectly evident that all the pioneers of socialism were compelled to depend upon democratic forces to implement their ideas, which were rooted in thoroughgoing internationalism. For Marx himself and for his closest followers, this was not a matter of convenience, but of conviction. In this respect, this little book attempts to honour various debts to Marx, and is not afraid to acknowledge them.

*   *   *

Most of these essays were first published in *Tribune*. Some have been run together, having appeared in different instalments. Otherwise they have not been greatly changed in the editing. I am grateful to Dick Clements and Douglas Hill for their persistent refusal to be discouraged by the bother some of them caused. When they printed some of these heresies, they caught a whole pack of troubles on my account. I sometimes felt that if everyone who had been moved to announce the cancellation of his or her subscription on my account had actually done so, I could have met my surviving co-readers in a very small room indeed, if not exactly in a telephone kiosk. The meeting would have been difficult to arrange, however. The fewer my colleagues remained, the more strongly they would have disagreed with one another. Fortunately, the *Tribune* habit was in practice quite difficult to kick, and the cancelled orders were usually themselves soon cancelled, so that I was able to give my due measure of offence to the same resigning readers over and again.

To meet the British left at its most infuriating and its most uplifting, in its most generous and its most crabbed frames of mind, one has only to follow those *Tribune* correspondence columns. There have been times when I have found these letter pages a rioting Rugby scrum of antagonised comrades, all boots and fervent hostility. On other occasions the same platform has been a singular outpost of freedom, from which one could speak when all the doors of the free press were locked, bolted and barred.

For those who love the left without romanticising it, and who are not afraid to follow the argument where it goes, such a newspaper is a priceless asset, whatever its follies, ennuis, and misjudgements may be.

*   *   *

The parts of this book were first published (sometimes in versions which were cut or sub-edited) in a number of different journals, but pre-eminently in *Tribune*. There follows a schedule. Several of these pieces were reprinted or translated, and some of them subsequently appeared in five or six different publications.

Chapter 1, Part I: *Tribune*, 28 June 1974. Part II: *Tribune*, 17 October 1980. Part III: *Tribune*, 24 May 1974. Part IV: *Tribune*, 3 October 1975.

Chapter 2, *Tribune*, 9 April 1976.

Chapter 3, Introduction to *Czechoslovakia and Socialism*, BRPF 1969.

Chapter 4, *Tribune*, 28 October 1977.

Chapter 5, *The Just Society*, Spokesman 1977.

Chapter 6, Part I: Foreword to Richard Day: *N.I. Bukharin, Selected Writings;* Part II: *Labour Leader,* November 1978.

Chapter 7, *Tribune*, 18 October 1974.

Chapter 8, Part I: *Tribune*, 23 November 1979. Part II: *Tribune,*

19 May 1978. Part III: *Tribune*, April 1978. Part IV: *Tribune*, 10 May 1974.

Chapter 9, Part I: *Tribune*, 2 July 1976. Part II: *Tribune*, 28 July 1978.

Chapter 10, *Tribune*, 20 October 1978.

Chapter 11, *Tribune*, 12 September 1980.

Chapter 12, *Laboratorio 1, Mondoperaio*, Rome 1979.

Chapter 13, *Labour Weekly*, 17 November 1978.

Chapter 14, Part I: *Spokesman* 1978. Part II: *Tribune*, 20 January 1978.

Chapter 15, *Tribune*, 26 September 1980.

Chapter 16, *Tribune*, 8 February 1979.

Chapter 17, *Socialism in the World*, 21, 1981.

Chapter 18, *Tribune*, February 1980.

Chapter 1

A Mirror to the Russias

I

A hundred years before Stalin died, Karl Marx published an article in the *New York Daily Tribune,* in which he touched on the question of crime and punishment. "It would be difficult", he wrote, "if not altogether impossible, to establish any principle upon which the justice or expediency of capital punishment could be founded, in a society glorying in its civilization. Punishment in general has been defended as a means either of ameliorating or of intimidating. Now what right have you to punish me for the amelioration or intimidation of others?" It is a good 'liberal' question, and Marx gave it a good 'liberal' answer: he pointed out that the French criminologist Quételet had, way back in 1829, accurately predicted "not only the amount, but all the different kinds of crimes committed in France in 1830", and that consequently crime was governed by objective causes producing regular effects. "Is there not", he asked, "a necessity for deeply reflecting upon an alteration of the system that breeds these crimes, instead of glorifying the hangman who executes a lot of criminals to make room only for the supply of new ones?"

The Russian October Revolution was led by men who hung on Marx's every word, and who indeed interrupted their concern with affairs of state in the midst of the most profound crises in order to arrange for the scholarly collection and publication of his writings. Early Soviet penal law, therefore, was haunted by these ideas. Until comparatively recently, the only careful study of Soviet forced labour was a work by two Menshevik historians, Dallin and Nikolaevsky. This book, published in the late forties, displayed no tendency to weakness in evaluating the deeds of the Bolsheviks, but it did contain a graphic chapter analyzing the early revolutionary ideas on crime and its suppression. Of course, a declared terror was in force during those days, against the political adversaries of the new regime.

Dallin and Nikolaevsky reported, "While Lenin was preaching suppression of political enemies, their conditions were actually incomparably better than they were under Lenin's successor, who professed humaneness and liberty". This state of affairs was clearly no liberal democracy, and Lenin shocked Bertrand Russell by his blunt advocacy of repression when they met in 1920. Yet there was, of course, a war on, and a brutal war at that, in which the enemies of the revolutionary State were often cruelty itself. Even so, alongside it, in the field of penology, the regime was positively utopian in its policies. The two Menshevik historians documented the hopes and the naivetés of these policies in a painstakingly factual account which is full of tragic overtones. On this matter, their view is far more objective than that of Aleksandr Solzhenitsyn, whose great book* sees only a continuous evolution between Lenin's Russia and Stalin's. They gave statistics for the (criminal) prison population:

1901	84,632
1903	96,005
1908	171,219
1912	183,949
1913	169,367
July 1917	24,095
1924	87,800
1925	148,000
1926	255,000
1927	198,000

It was obvious that, political terror apart, the new society's troubles still offered abundant work for a Soviet Quételet to do. Indeed, the old tsarist prisons were full by the mid-twenties and after Lenin's death they were soon bursting at the seams, so that space could not be found in them for large numbers of sentenced criminals. The institution of parole 'became a means for relieving the situation'. During 1925-26 only 36 per cent of all sentences imposed were actually carried out. In facing this situation, the Soviet government intensified the experimental development of penal colonies. Here, according to the Men-

*The Gulag Archipelago by Aleksandr Solzhenitsyn. New York: Harper & Row, 1974.

sheviks, were the seeds of the Gulag Archipelago, that vast chain of soul-grinding concentration camps which was forged during the following years. Whole Londons were sent to live there, while there were times when whole Rutlands would be executed within short periods. Needless to say, a Soviet Quételet could not possibly have foreseen the totals and proportions of the 'crime' waves which would swell these new institutions, in their turn, to bursting point. Social indicators alone do not allow us to predict the extent of individual capriciousness in an all-powerful tyrant.

Aleksandr Solzhenitsyn was a victim of that horrendous outgrowth. He only served part of his term in a general labour camp, and believes he would have remained among the un-counted dead there if he had not fibbed on an official form, stating that his occupation was 'nuclear physicist'. The result was that he was sent for a large part of his time to a 'special workshop' of the kind described so movingly in *The First Circle*. Solzhenitsyn is an honest commentator. He entered imprison-ment on the heels of millions (yes, some millions) of predecessors. This dossier contains case histories submitted by spokesmen of many different generations of prisoners, sucked into gulag in successive waves of frenzied repression. He enumerates these waves, involving the longer series of purges, and the deportation of whole communities of peasants and en-tire nationalities. Many of the stories told by the witnesses and participants involved confirm others long known in the West, but many are new, and all are terrible.

For the Soviet press to claim that the work is simultaneously a slander and that it contains nothing new, is manifestly absurd, and the test of this absurdity is quite simple: Why not allow the author to publish the work at home at his own expense, if no publishing house dare take the commercial risk? While Solzhenitsyn's arguments may (indeed, in some cases, should) be contested, the factual basis upon which they rest is beyond reasonable challenge. *Gulag Archipelago* will yet become a best-seller in Russia, and solely because of the solid core of truth it contains. This truth will not be indefinitely suppressed, if only because rational choices are not open to a people who deprive themselves of their own history, and no nation can remain irra-tional indefinitely. But such a truth carries with it also a cold rage, because the murdering viciousness of the State it unmasks exceeded, to the nth degree, all the little excesses of the bourgeois hangmen whom Marx had so passionately denounced, and indeed most of those of their more bloodthirsty successors whom Marx never lived to see. It is an open question, perhaps, who has killed most communists in history. Some would nominate Hitler, but only because racial prejudice leaves Indonesia out of the record. Yet in all probability Stalin equalled even that awesome tally. And alongside the communists, Stalin also caught up the millions of innocents: the old professors and the eight-year-old girls whose fathers were dragged off before their eyes, the Tartars, the Chechens, the Volga Germans, the priests and the victims of low-level GPU jealousies, the geneticists and the engineers. Not all died of exposure and overwork, but uncountable numbers did. Even the numbers of those deliberately shot are almost limitless.

All those State crimes needed State criminals to perpetrate them, and sadists of all degrees came forward at Stalin's command, often subsequently to roast on their own spit at that same fearful caprice. Pitifully few of the torturers and murderers have been tried, and most of those in private. Arch-villains in the whole process still pass out their days in superannuation, as respected servants of society. Solzhenitsyn is undoubtedly right that the record must be published, and the main culprits called to account. He suggests that no penalty need be exacted from them, beyond the evaluation and publication of their past misdeeds, and this seems particularly Marxian in its view of the nature of punishment.

It is quite manifest that this book is already a key document in Russian history, inasmuch as it begins to impose this penalty of knowledge. Only such a document, it should be added, can explain the enigma of Solzhenitsyn himself: a vast man, with profoundly humane sympathies and a colossal range of understanding, who entered prison life as a Marxist critical of Stalin, and left it declaring himself a Christian mystic. In the West this conversion is sometimes seen as the triumph of individual conscience over totalitarianism. But in the future, hopefully, juster terrain, it may well be seen as the revenge of totalitarianism on individual conscience.

Certainly, Solzhenitsyn has been shaped in prison, as he constantly informs us. This has ennobled him and degraded him at the same time. His hatred of Russian tyranny is entirely understandable and just. But this does not excuse his very mistaken assumptions that Mother Russia has a monopoly on all villainy, that the only real repression is Russian repression, and that injustice came into the world, fully formed, in October 1917. In passing he describes a particularly nasty atrocity in Kolyma, and then adds the footnote: "say there, Bertrand Russell's 'War Crimes Tribunal'! Why don't you use this bit of material? Or doesn't it suit you?" But the Russell Tribunal drew attention to war crimes in Vietnam, by detailed and scholarly investigation and reportage, against the hostility of most of the Western press and the calculated indifference of the Soviet leadership. Its proceedings were scantily reported in the USSR, and official communism outside Vietnam and Cuba largely ostracised it. Why? In part, for sure, because both Russell himself, and many of the jurors he chose, had a lifelong record of hostility to Stalin's atrocities and were not only acutely disturbed by the then growing symptoms of 're-Stalinisation', but were saying so.

When Solzhenitsyn, in the Russian edition of the second volume of this work, condemns Russell and the Dean of Canterbury in the same breath as apologists for the Russia of Gulag, he reveals his very large ignorance of the outside world. Russell not only denounced the Stalin terror, but could not abide the unspeakable Dean, partly because he was a mendacious Stalinist propagandist, and partly because he was a luminary of the Church of England. He saw both the institutions as mind-benders in a reactionary cause, but did not find it altogether surprising that Establishment should speak for establishment, and Church for church. Yet in attacking such a target, Solzhenitsyn is really acting on the algebraic formula, a friend of my friend is my friend, and an enemy of my enemy is my friend. That's alright with symbols, but not with people, and still less so with human collectives, especially when these embrace nations and States. The real allies in the West of the cause of democracy in Russia will be precisely those who are most concerned about Vietnam, Cambodia, and Chile, while the men of Watergate could show themselves willing to trade every free Russian spirit, quite gladly, for a modest piece of the action in exploiting Soviet trade opportunities. Freedom, Aleksandr Solzhenitsyn will soon discover in his exile, is indivisible, and, alas, it is still no less a subversive principle in the 'free' world than it is elsewhere.

Speaking at the 22nd Congress of the Soviet Communist Party, Nikita Khrushchev, after returning in public to the harrowing theme he had already elaborated in private two Congresses earlier, asked a question which his stenographers wrote down without a question mark: "Perhaps", he said, "we should erect a monument in Moscow to perpetuate the memory of the comrades who fell victim to arbitrary rule."

In Moscow, a decade and a half further on, no such monument has yet appeared. Khrushchev himself has two monuments, though: one a 'dissident' sculpture by Ernst Niezvestny, erected over his grave as a gesture of solidarity with what Khrushchev might have been; and the other, two long volumes of rambling memoirs, dictated onto tape from an old man's recollections, and transcribed by hostile Sovietologists in the United States for diffusion by a capitalist publishing house. Stalin was removed from his bed alongside the stuffed remains of Lenin, and cemented under a thick jacket of reinforced concrete by the Kremlin Wall. It would have seemed perfectly reasonable had the ceremony been accompanied by the transfixion of the corpse's heart with an appropriate stake, and the recitation of relevant psalms of exorcism. Instead, a macabre moonlit flit was done, and bits that are left of the monster now lie somewhere under a plain slab marked 'Stalin', which is as near as Khrushchev ever got to honouring the dead of the great Soviet purges in any form of monumental art.

But for all that, their monument is now complete, and a staggering size and mass it has. Solzhenitsyn's *Gulag* is a truly extraordinary work, which beyond doubt will soon become visible all over the USSR, even though it has been set up in print in enforced exile. Solzhenitsyn, of course, mourns least of all the 'comrades' but writes passionately of all the other legions of victims who fell into the forced labour system. Even so, those without the benefit of factional allegiance will think from his evidence that the suffering was generally shared, and that communists bore their due share of it.

II

Varlam Shalamov had some unfortunate literary opinions in 1937, when he was thirty years old. He approved of Bunin, the

Nobel Prizewinner who, he ill-advisedly declared, was "a classic author of Russian literature". Consequently Shalamov was arrested, and thenceforward spent 17 years in prison camps, most of which were located in the Kolyma area, in which perished vast numbers of detainees. Released in 1954, he was subsequently able to publish poetry, and gained a reputation in his own country as a writer of nature-loving verse. But these particular stories* of life in Kolyma, while they remain beautifully sensitive to the flora and fauna, are not publishable in the Soviet Union, because they chronicle the doings of men. It is said that Solzhenitsyn sought out Shalamov as a collaborator when he began work on the *Gulag Archipelago,* but that Shalamov declined.

The result is these stories, selected, apparently, from a very much richer collection which has been published in the Russian language by emigre presses. John Glad, the translator, has provided a version which reads far better than the crass journalese into which much of *Gulag* has been rendered for English-speaking readers. He has also provided a foreword, in which he claims, I think rightly, that Shalamov "is too major a writer to be ignored".

The hardships of Kolyma, where permafrost binds the earth, and where greed for gold provoked the workers' state to spend the lives of men and women as if they were confetti, were documented with gruesome effect by Dallin and Nikolaevsky in their book. More recently they have been carefully elaborated by Robert Conquest in a small book which appeared in 1978. But Shalamov gives the feel of the place, with a quality of compassion which is truly extraordinary. Much of his writing concerns the daily life of the convicts: the ordeal of the bathhouse: the constant struggle for a crust to eat: the bruising toil. "Pity for animals returned earlier than pity for people", he tells us. When Solzhenitsyn shows us a two-class universe in Gulag, with the common criminals terrorising the 'politicals', Shalamov gives us a far more nuanced picture. True, some of the criminals are brutish in the most abandoned way: but others are not. There is a touching account of how film scriptwriter Platonov became a storyteller in the camp, thus winning protection from the thugs he entertained.

Kolyma Tales. Varlam Shalamov. Norton 1980.

One amazing story describes what happened when the first wartime lease-lend bulldozer was delivered to Kolyma, and the machine grease which came with it was devoured by the hungry inmates. It was thought that the dozer would be put to construction work, moving logs. But no. It went instead to re-fashion a grave. "A stone pit stuffed full with corpses of 1938 was sliding down the hill, revealing the secret of Kolyma. In Kolyma bodies are not given over to earth, but to stone. Stone keeps secrets and reveals them. The permafrost keeps and reveals secrets. All of our loved ones . . . all those who were shot, beaten to death, sucked dry by starvation, can still be recognised after tens of years. There were no gas furnaces in Kolyma. The corpses wait in stone, in the permafrost".

In 1938, dying work gangs had slaved to shape these stone pits. But after six years, earth movements opened the grave, and corpses began to slide down the mountainside. So the bulldozer found its vocation: it

"scraped up the frozen bodies, thousands of bodies of thousands of skeleton-like corpses. Nothing had decayed . . ."

at the end of its labours, all were decently re-interred.

"And then I remembered the greedy blaze of the fireweed, the furious blossoming of the taiga in Summer when it tried to hide in the grass and foliage any deed of man — good or bad. And if I forget, the grass will forget. But the permafrost and stone will not forget."

Shalamov did not, in fact forget, and nor must we.

III

Karl Marx was very fond of Balzac, and Lenin had a positive reverence for Tolstoy. Paul Lafargue tells us that Marx's admiration for Balzac was "so profound that he had planned to write a criticism of *La Comédie Humaine* as soon as he should have finished his economic studies". Lenin's own powerful sympathy for Tolstoy is made clear in a whole series of articles, at least one of which still bears reading: It is called *Leo Tolstoy as the Mirror of the Russian Revolution,* and it begins with a very wise question:

"To identify the name of a great artist with the revolution, which he has obviously failed to understand and from which he had obviously alienated himself, may at first seem strange and artificial. How, indeed, can one describe as a mirror that which does not reflect things correctly?''

Yet nonetheless, although Lenin's philosophy was worlds apart from Tolstoy's, the revolutionary could not fail to see in the work of the novelist a 'world significance', reflecting 'the world significance of the Russian Revolution'. In exactly the same way, the Balzac whom Marx held in such affection was, in his political allegiance, an almost pure reactionary.

That dwindling band of apologists who maintain that every baseness of the modern Russian government is a signpost to worldwide brotherhood should refresh their memories of these facts, for the plain truth is that the case of Alexandr Solzhenitsyn makes them all topical again. Beyond doubt Solzhenitsyn is a writer who connects on the same plane as Balzac and Tolstoy, whose novels, as Georg Lukacs recognised, not only embody the best traditions of realism, but at the same time demand to be placed among the great artistic achievements of the twentieth century. They could fulfill the second of these claims without meeting the first, but the fact that they combine them both means that it is perfectly reasonable to see Solzhenitsyn, just as Lenin saw Tolstoy, as a "mirror of the Russian Revolution". Critical realism is not a literary style to be affected, but a commitment to the preservation of living truths, which has frequently in the past set the output of great writers at odds with their own strenuously advocated professions of belief. Whether we look into *The Human Comedy* or into *War and Peace,* we find infinitely more than the patchwork of prejudices which made up their authors' creeds. Marxist critics like Lucien Goldmann have repeatedly discussed this phenomenon. For the benefit of both Stalinist backwoodsmen and the hierarchs of the liberal establishment, it needs to be explained again in relation to *Cancer Ward* and *The First Circle.* It also, alas, needs to be understood when one reads the latest Solzhenitsyn work, the *Letter to Soviet Leaders*.*

In this tract we can hear again the accents of the querulous Tolstoy, advocating abstinence and asceticism. Solzhenitsyn doesn't stop here, adding zero growth and deference to a de-

*Letter to Soviet Leaders from A. Solzhenitsyn. London: Collins & Harvill in association with Index on Censorship. 1974.

ideologised party elite, which have the effect of bringing the mixture into phase with some current vogues in the West. A veritable quacks' chorus has arisen in the liberal press to tell us how profound this all is, and how *Russian*. Yes, it is Russian all right — part of the same Great-Russian nonsense which underpins all the dreadful conservatism of the Soviet authorities, and inimical to that free and cosmopolitan Russian spirit which made both 1917 and the richly humane contributions of Solzhenitsyn's own vast novels. When Tolstoy died, a liberal commentator wrote of him, in an obituary celebration, "How majestic, how mighty, a figure cast in a single piece of pure metal, stands this Tolstoy . . . this living incarnation of the integral principle."

"Uph", snorted Lenin, "eloquent talk but it is all untrue. The figure of Tolstoy is neither in a single piece, nor in a pure piece, nor even in metal. And it was *not* for his 'integrity' but precisely because of his departure from integrity that all these bourgeois admirers rose in honour of his memory."

Solzhenitsyn's pamphlet gets some things right, of course. The use of the motor car *does* threaten Russia, just as it is already ruining England. The sale of Soviet natural gas and oil to the United States might be very good for President Nixon or his successors but it won't be an unmixed blessing either for Russia or for the rest of the world. A war with China *would* be a disaster, although it would hardly be, as Solzhenitsyn sees it, purely an ideological battle — the Soviet government maintains huge forces on the Chinese frontier for material reasons as well as mental ones, and it did not invade Czechoslovakia in order to reinforce a reading of dialectical materialism, but in order to maintain the hold of a very material power structure over the USSR itself. When he outlines his platform of ecological conservatism, Solzhenitsyn's proposals are particularly hairy — the settlement of North Eastern Russia isn't at all an attractive proposition in present circumstances, which may not prevent Mr Brezhnev from contemplating it.

But the worst feature of the Solzhenitsyn scheme of things is that it completely writes off the struggle for democracy, and aspires only to the creation of a benevolent despotism liberated from dogma. No modern despot can be benevolent, and this is most of the real trouble in modern Russia. No man or group of men can assimilate the necessary feedback, leave alone stimulate the necessary feedback, to direct the political and economic destinies of a contemporary state without creating the most memorable disasters. However painful and slow it may be, democracy is the only institution which can call forth that degree of social insight which complex economic collectives need to adjust their policies. That Soviet democracy will not have to face the problems of fundamental class conflicts does not in the least mean that all personal and group interests are identical, or that all are in the short-run readily to be reconciled. What democracy can do for the Soviet Union, and what autocracy, however benign, will never do, is to make this divergence of interests into a constructive social force, instead of driving it underground. Disfranchised, it seeds apathy and withdrawal, and rots away at the morale of the entire body politic. Needless to say, such a reborn democracy will not need either a stock exchange, or a war with China, or a House of Lords. We saw the beginnings of its outline in the Prague Spring, and surely, given time, a Moscow Spring is on its way.

IV

Toleration is, of course, a Good Thing, even if we usually find it easier to tolerate our enemies from a distance than it is to put up with our friends when they're close by. Religious toleration rarely issues from profound religious belief, although in our own heroic Cromwellian past it once did, and we should remember the fact with due pride. More normally it correlates with a certain scepticism, as Gibbon slyly told us: "The various modes of worship which prevailed in the Roman world, were all considered by the people as equally true; by the philosophers, as equally false; and by the magistrate, as equally useful."

A uniquely useful feature of most authentic schools of Christianity in this respect has been the splendidly disciplinarian doctrine of hellfire, refined as an instrument of social control subtle beyond the dreams of the Ancients, and hardly since rivalled in theology, though all too often rivalled in the practical behaviour of modern States. In bygone years, with hell on its side, the secular authority was on a sure-fire winner, to coin a phrase. Not without justice does Christopher Hill claim that "Theories of democracy rose as hell declined". This grisly feat of the Christian imagination has meant that, although humanist heresies, and regrettable attempts to establish God's Kingdom here on Earth have not been absolutely excluded (so that we owe to men schooled in Christianity a series of memorable humane impulses from the epoch of the Putney debates down to the courageous witness of Camillo Torres) for the most part the Church has been firmly on the side of law and order. Indeed, the meaner the order and the more unjust the law, the greater supporting force of Christian 'morality'. Notable economies in the salaries of the constabulary are possible when the citizens believe that all their most rational and spontaneous desires and endeavours are, if unbridled, liable to cause them to fry forever in God's own sulphurous furnace.

So if anyone likes people, and thinks that they might conceivably be good, he is likely to tangle with the Priesthood, possibly before and certainly not long after he has fallen out with the magistracy. Nowhere has this been more true than in Holy Russia, where official religion was even more official, and even more disgusting, than it has traditionally been in the West. The Russian Orthodox Church was a conspiracy against the people, against decency, and against any kind of humane behaviour. We rightly remember it in the image of Rasputin, the sham monk who secreted himself like a monstrous tapeworm in the deranged brain of the czarina, before both parasite and host were brought to a dreadful end. This symbol perfectly captures the merger of 'spiritual' and secular functions which has been the badge of Orthodoxy ever since the original Council of Nicocea was followed by the rigorous persecution of all who dissented at its deliberations.

Arguably the nastiest of the many vices of this very vicious institution was its capability to mutate and corrupt the social forms assumed even by the apparently antithetical doctrine which was to replace it. This mutation was possible only in the unique context of Russian society.

"The Church", wrote Trotsky, "never rose to that commanding height which it attained in the Catholic West: it was satisfied with the role of spiritual servant of the autocracy, and counted this a recompense for its humility. The bishops and metropolitans enjoyed authority merely as deputies of the temporal power. The patriarchs were changed along with the czars . . . Two hundred thousand priests and monks were in all essentials a part of the bureaucracy, a sort of police of the gospel."

To the extent that there is truth in this polemic description, we must next face the almost inconceivable fact that, nearly 60 years after the overthrow of czardom, serious intellectuals apparently wish to revive the old order with all its superstitious underpinning. That indeed is exactly what Aleksandr Solzhenitsyn's latest book, written by a team of religious dissenters, advocates.

From Under the Rubble* is almost unreadable, and it could never have been published if Solzhenitsyn's artistic reputation and commercial success had not previously been established at a truly remarkable threshold. It is said that huge advances have been paid for this work: if this is true, we should not be surprised if the liquidator is soon observed paying a long visit to Collins/Harvill and their American opposite numbers. Of course, some difficult books repay study, and tiny minorities can be right. But in this case, all that Solzhenitsyn has found in his rubbish heap is unadulterated rubbish: at the level of argument it is dishonest to an extraordinary degree, and at the level of ideas it is entirely vacuous. Solzhenitsyn advocates the displacement of the Soviet establishment by a new Orthodoxy, an elite band based on preposterous gibberish. The evidence for the desirability of this new dawn of obscurantism appears to rest on the propositions that elites are very necessary, and that medieval churches were better built than modern skyscrapers, which last contention few will deny. But pyramids in Egypt and Mexico have proved even more durable than cathedrals, and no-one can doubt the sturdy security of the elitism which prospered while they were being erected. Why shouldn't we all be Aztecs then? In that way we could improve upon the anaemic substitutions of the Mass by holding convivial cannibal feasts.

Solzhenitsyn opens his work with a scurrilous attack on Sakharov, who is himself a fairly conservative liberal, one of whose shortcomings, it seems, is the advocacy of intellectual freedom. "Much good this has done the West", says our Prophet. His introduction to the book is followed by a long item contributed by a pious, if not too scrupulous, fellow called Shafarevich, which is quite the silliest polemic against the very idea of socialism ever written in recent decades. Shafarevich quotes Marx's strictures on various schools of early 'socialism' as if they were Marx's own ideas, and goes on to found a

*From Under the Rubble. A. Solzhenitsyn. Collins/Harvill 1975.

hypothetical universal death-wish on the words of an old patriotic song. After this revelation, F. Korsakov tells us that the Lord chastises those he loves, and draws from this premise the conclusions (a) that all chastisement comes from the Lord and (b) that since chastisement has not been wanting in the USSR the Lord's love must correlate directly. Most of us wouldn't wish to bet on that.

How could it come about that such nostrums could be seriously canvassed in a modern age? First, we must acknowledge a cardinal fact about recent Russian society: its appalling heritage of backwardness. Political and industrial revolutions, social revolutions even, cannot simply leap over the cultural traditions against which they react. In the old Russian world, religion had a vital role; and not only because it offered the fear of eternal punishment: it also offered "the flowers that bedecked the chains". Secondly, the 'modernisation' process unleashed terrible repressions which gave even greater scope to elements of that atavism; in the traumatic world of Gulag, the flowers could come to seem more, not less important as the chains got heavier. Ignorance could sometimes cope better than intelligence with the irrationalities of this terrible world. Bigoted priests might well resist where free-thinking socialists and communists could not. This had nothing much to do with the strength of ideas, but a great deal to do with the weakness of the flesh. If one believed in a literal hell which would engulf all compromisers, and a literal heaven which would embrace all true believers, one was in a better position to be intransigent than those who anticipated that dead was dead, and injured was injured, and humiliation was simply the result of the application of a brutal power. The rooted conviction that the next world would always go one worse than this present would imply that, the worse the terror of the actual State, the more devastating and horrendous would be God's final wrath to come, if one rendered unto Ceasar anything which really belonged to God.

But the fear is not the reality, anymore than the wish. If cruelty by men could establish the truth of God's heavenly kingdom, the argument would have been resolved long ago, and not only in Russia. Instead, the evidence moves all the other way. If one assumes this life is the only one, it seems sensible to make it bearable. Experience shows that democratic societies are less intolerable than authoritarian ones. On the other hand, while it remains not at all proven that socialism is incompatible with very far-reaching democracy, we would all be grateful for some hard positive evidence from present day socialisms. Such evidence, were it to develop, would not please these authors. On the contrary, they believe that the very rigours of Soviet repression have guaranteed the spiritual health of their countrymen.

To be sure, no genuine socialist democracy would need to forbid these latest writings of Solzhenitsyn, although their publication would be limited since so few would wish to read them. Yet we need to face the last great enigma posed by this puzzling man: which is not how he could personally develop such strange opinions, but how the social occasion in which they flourish could survive. The opinions themselves are obviously no remedy for the ills of the Soviet Society, but they *are* part of its disease, and will likely persist until this is understood.

Chapter 2

Sakharov's Country and our World

In his book, *My Country and the World,** Academician
Sakharov devotes a whole chapter to "the liberal intelligentsia
of the West", the main gist of which is a criticism of what he
terms "Leftist-liberal faddishness".

Sakharov is moved to write about this by various silly attitudes which have been reported to him, such as those of the
French Communist sympathiser who asked his mother-in-law
whether "there was a particle of truth" in Solzhenitsyn's
account of Gulag. Sakharov's reaction is understandable. But,
as so often happens, the credulity of some Westerners about
Soviet affairs is matched by a similar naïveté among some
Russians about the West.

The trusting and innocent response is by no means surprising:
if one has come to disbelieve in the innate virtue of one's own
establishment, it is easy enough, in rejecting it, to embrace an
alternative, warts and all. Yet Sakharov himself would obviously like to rise above the Tweedledum and Tweedledee cold-war
imperatives, and, in an attempt to uphold his belief in universal
human rights, he specifically condemns the ill-treatment of
political prisoners in Indonesia, among other places.

It is all the more damaging and inconsistent of him to move
from such a (well-justified) commitment to the view that the
American government is, or ought to behave as, the leader of the
'free world'. Because Academician Sakharov is not alone
amongst honest men in holding that view, it is instructive to ask,
what are the connections between political prisoners in Indonesia and the 'leaders of the free world'?

A recent study throws a great deal of light on this question.**
It may not be generally known that the most careful estimates

*   Collins/Harvill, 1975.
** *Ten Years' Military Terror in Indonesia,* Spokesman, 1975.

put the number of Indonesian political detainees at around 100,000, or ten times Amnesty's most recent guess at the number of politically dissident prisoners in the Soviet Union.

Indonesian prisoners are graded into three categories. Category A prisoners (some 1,500) are alleged to be awaiting trial on charges of complicity in the events of October 1965. Categories B and C, the remainder, are either detained without any prospect of trial as "security risks", or described by the authorities as "awaiting release". They have been awaiting it a long time.

All the evidence agrees that all these detainees are held in conditions which are far below any civilised minimum standards. (See Carmel Budiardjo's study in the *Spokesman* volume). So, if the population of Indonesia is about half that of the Soviet Union, then Indonesia is approximately 20 times worse than the Soviet Union on the straightforward index of wrongful imprisonment of political critics.

But that is only the beginning of the question. The government which maintains these huge penal colonies for political dissidents did not arrive in office easily, and would have needed to build additional prisons from four to ten times larger than those which already exist, if it had not avoided this necessity by the simple expedient of massacre. No one will ever know exactly how many people were butchered in Suharto's coup: the smallest estimate is 400,000, and it is commonly and credibly claimed that the real figure was nearer one million.

In the meagre newspaper coverage which this bloodstorm received in the West, it was reported that the rivers of Java were blocked by the bodies of the victims.

It is at this point that the new evidence should interest Academician Sakharov. In a painstaking study *(Exporting Military-Economic Development,* in the *Spokesman* volume), Peter Dale Scott has now shown us, blow by blow, exactly how the Central Intelligence Agency plotted the downfall of the Sukarno regime, prepared the Indonesian military for insurrection, and arranged, through the Ford Foundation's good offices, for the training of the necessary civilian cadres to take over the subsequent administration. Indonesia's terror, in short, was made in Washington.

Nor is Indonesia the only blackspot in Amnesty's books. Iran, for instance, is a personal dictatorship of the most unsavoury species. The Shah rules through a private security force, the Savak, which used means which have long since been denied to the KGB to enforce political order. Political murders are common, and administrative executions quite frequent.

Sakharov has a good deal to say about the conditions of the Kurds in Iraq. However, not only the Kurds, but all national minorities in Iran, are violently suppressed.

In what circumstances did the Shah's repressive regime originate? The recent disclosures in Washington make this perfectly plain: it all began in America, with some useful assistance from British Intelligence and the late Herbert Morrison. In the same way, the torturers of Brazil and Chile owe not only their power, but, all too often, their actual techniques and training, to the appropriate sub-departments of the CIA.

That a variant form of liberal democracy, more or less unscathed, rules in America itself, remains true. But if one ignores the connections of Empire, one sees this in an altogether artificial light.

It is this fact, a key one, which makes Sakharov's judgment about Vietnam so outrageously wide of the mark. Was there a simple alternative in Vietnam between communist autocracy and liberal democracy? Clearly there was not: the succession of puppet governments established in South Vietnam (or South Korea) by the Americans were neither liberal nor democratic. They were corrupt and self-seeking conspiracies against their own peoples.

One doesn't need to read the publications of the Democratic Republic of Vietnam to understand this: it is sufficiently apparent from such sources as Graham Greene's novel *The Quiet American,* which is all the more telling for its sympathetic understanding of the background and *mores* of the American personnel who were involved.

If Western intellectuals do not wish to see the growth of freedom of expression and personal and civil rights in Asia, as Sakharov charges, then they err gravely. But Sakharov himself errs equally gravely if he remains indifferent to the question of imperialism, which means recurrent starvation throughout the Third World, enforced underdevelopment coupled with distorted development, and a dependent condition based on widespread servitude and equally generalised oppression. The hungry are not free.

Sakharov, in seeking international support for creative

freedom, is looking in the wrong place. Empires sustain only those freedoms they find compatible with dominion. In the modern age, only the socialist culture has the requisite breadth and vitality to defend and advance the cause of liberty as a good in itself, without deference to partial national or imperial interests and without equivocation.

It is not an accident that a liberal 'moderate' like Lord Chalfont makes television programmes about the enlightenment of the Shah of Persia, or that Henry Kissinger remains unmoved by the evidence of his handiwork in Chile or Brazil. England has an oil deficit, and America a 'sphere of influence'.

Of course, it is always possible to opt for the traditional view of the cold war, as has Aleksandr Solzhenitsyn. In this case, one either doesn't worry about electric shock treatment in South American prisons, or one says that Leonid Plyushch should rot in jail for rocking the boat.

But anyone who looks at the repression which exists, around the world, with anything like an impartial eye, is bound to observe that the imprisonment of a few thousand more Chileans or Indonesians does nothing whatever to relax the regime endured by Vladimir Bukovsky in Russia. On the contrary, freedom is indivisible in the modern world, and must be defended against all who abuse it, whomever they serve.

In this connection it is difficult to exaggerate the significance of the movement of opinion in the West European communist parties, which are now openly speaking out, not only against repression in Chile or South Africa, but also against injustice in the Soviet Union. Late in 1975, the French and Italian Communists published an important joint declaration, which affirmed their common acceptance of a number of very clear democratic commitments.

Soon afterwards, the French Communists began an altercation with the Soviet authorities on the question of 'Labour camps', brought into public scrutiny by a BBC television interview with Academician Sakharov himself. When 2,000 mathematicians launched an appeal for Leonid Plyushch, the 'dissident' Soviet mathematician, this triggered off a mass rally in the Mutualité in Paris, and the French Communist Party then decided to intervene in the case. Now Plyushch is at liberty, recuperating from his enforced 'treatment' in a psychiatric unit.

Since Sakharov wrote his book, John Gollan has added a

British communist voice to this encouraging ferment.* Gollan offers a long analysis of the whole period since the 20th Congress of the Communist Party of the Soviet Union, now (incredibly it seems) 20 years behind us. He makes a serious effort to remain constructive and measured in his criticisms of current repressive measures in the Soviet Union, but at the same time he chronicles some extremely grave derelictions.

"Khrushchev's so-called secret report", he tells us, "was a courageous act." In 1956, there were many prominent people in the communist movement who denied the authenticity of this report, so that this is a statement the utterance of which itself required a certain resolution.

More, Gollan goes on to cite, without adverse comment, Roy Medvedev's major history of Stalinism, *Let History Judge.***
He also makes extensive use of the work of Jean Ellenstein, the interesting French communist historian.

For all the welcome advances registered in this statement, it would still be most interesting to hear the comments of Soviet dissidents upon it. "The democracy had to develop", Gollan writes, "but Stalin's regime held back this development, distorted it, retarded it, and even partially reversed it." These seem rather mild words, when we read earlier on that "Stalin personally initialled some 44,000 death sentences".

If we followed John Gollan's advice, and referred to Roy Medvedev's history, we would find, further, that not only tens, but indeed hundreds, of thousands were executed, while millions were deported. What can survive of the most rudimentary democratic forms in such a moral hurricane must surely be minimal indeed. Sakharov might certainly be impatient of such a temperate judgment, and Roy Medvedev, who would understand Gollan's caution, might well be able to set the whole matter in a clearer light.

For all that, the Gollan statement represents part of a healthy evolution. While the communists of Western Europe are belatedly standing up to be counted, however, the same cannot be said for the most powerful of their (and our) opponents. Detente or not, Henry Kissinger still seems to think he has more right to appoint the Italian government than does the Italian people, and everywhere that the Left gains strength, the CIA

*Marxism Today, January 1976.
**Spokesman, 1976.

dollars somehow seem to flow unabated, whether Congress approves or not.

If John Gollan has not yet said his last word on Soviet democracy, neither, for certain, has Academician Sakharov finally uncovered the ultimate reality of the 'free world'.

Chapter 3

Spring is Sprung

On 21 August, 1968, five nations claiming to be "socialist" invaded a sixth nation, also claiming to be socialist. When half a million troops from the Soviet Union, Hungary, Poland, Bulgaria, and the German Democratic Republic moved into Czechoslovakia, it was not only a series of solemn pledges under treaty which were broken. The plain fact is that all six governments concerned not only laid claim to pursue, in general, socialist policies: they each also laid claim to be representative of social structures which, in broad outline, had already evolved to embody "socialism". Was "socialism", then, beginning to savage itself? Were "socialist" countries no less prone to intimidate one another than their capitalist forbears?

One would search in vain through the writings of Marx, Engels, Lenin, Stalin, Trotsky, Luxemburg, Mao Tse-Tung, or whomsoever else in the socialist pantheon might readily be invoked, in order to find analysis of this sort of situation. There is no consideration, in the classic literature of Marxism, of the problems of military strategy in conflicts between socialist states. Bluntly, the originators of socialist doctrine would have regarded such eventualities as inconceivable. Indeed for a society which has truly overcome the exploitation of man by man, such an eventuality *is* out of the question. This assumption is basic to the socialist tradition, and of course it pre-dates Karl Marx. But it was perfectly clearly said by him in the First Address which he drafted on behalf of the International Workingmen's Association to outline its policy on the Franco-Prussian War:

> "In contrast to old society, with its economical miseries and political delirium, a new society is springing up whose international rule will be *Peace*, because its national ruler will be — everywhere the same — *Labour!*"

This thought has been expressed in more general terms: "A

people which enslaves others forges its own chains", said Marx again: and it has been amplified:

"The victorious proletariat can force no blessings of any kind upon any foreign nation without undermining its own victory by so doing", wrote Engels. It has also been elaborated, with deadly specificity, by Lenin:

> "The social and political character of war is determined not by the 'good intentions' of individuals or groups, or even of peoples, but by the position of the *class* which conducts the war, by the class *policy* of which the war is a continuation . . ."

For the world communist movement, the invasion of Czechoslovakia therefore raises some fundamental questions. Either the assumptions of a century and a half of socialist thought are invalid, or there exist unsocialist elements *deep in the structure* of the socialist countries which initiated the invasion.

There is no way to avoid this dilemma. Although it is possible to maintain that the movement of half a million troops into another country, the arrest of its Governmental leaders, and the subsequent imposition upon them of political options which were not their own, is not an act of war, such a claim is no more convincing than the parliamentary evasions of Mr Anthony Eden, who claimed that the British bombardment of Port Said did not indicate that there was in progress anything so untoward as a war with Egypt, but merely revealed that there existed a state of "armed conflict". Baldly, we can state with certainty that Karl Marx would have found such actions, whether they were styled as acts of war or not, indicative of the existence of grave social tensions within the nations that initiated them.

It is widely understood that the People's Republic of Czechoslovakia was not, in fact, at the time of the action, reverting to pre-socialist political or economic norms. The dispatches of the *Morning Star's* reporter in Prague provided one vein of evidence on this score. So does the fact that opinion polls in Czechoslovakia revealed that more than 95 per cent of the population were actively in favour of the continued socialisation of their economy. But even if Czechoslovakia had been in fact "reverting to capitalism", as it manifestly was *not*, there is ample textual evidence in the writings of, for instance, both Engels and Lenin, to indicate that they, at any rate, would have opposed military intervention of the type which occurred on 21 August. The Chinese People's Republic is led by men who believe, somewhat quaintly, that capitalism is being restored in the Soviet Union. By analogy with the action of the Warsaw Pact powers, they could justify sending their armies to Moscow in order to reorganise its affairs. Stalin believed that not merely capitalism, but indeed fascism, had been re-established in Yugoslavia after 1948. Had he then betrayed his principles by refusing to act in the manner now established by his successors? Since the vogue in Moscow, among the influential members of the ruling caucus, seems to be towards the rehabilitation of the Generalissimo, it might be useful if they would ponder on that question.

Of course, as an accompaniment of wars, one inevitably meets lies. Liars flourish behind the lines of battle as at no other times. Lies, particularly lies told in pursuance of public duty by state spokesmen, are themselves a classic indicator of underlying social tensions, and of suppressed social conflicts. An orgy of official lies accompanied the movement of troops into Prague. Almost a year after the invasion, the persons who were alleged to have invited the Soviet authorities to intervene in order to save Czech socialism, have still not come forward. Indeed, those eminent Czech and Slovak opponents of the new upsurge of socialist democracy who were nominated, by general rumour, for this honour, have since been publicly exculpated from the thought, by Mr Husak's Government. It is, it appears, a gross reflection upon their honour, to say nothing of their nationality, to suggest that they would implicate themselves in any such treason. When the immediate given justification for the intervention has proved so absurdly unfounded, what more need be said about the more extravagant lies, which were told afterwards, concerning arms caches, enemy "tourists" and the like?

When the subjugation of socialist democracy began, after the August days, European socialists had a manifest duty of solidarity with their colleagues in the Czechoslovak trade unions and Communist Party. They had to resist, strongly, both the disgraceful pressures of the Western Governments, such as the British Labour administration, to use the fact of the invasion as a pretext for strengthening NATO: and at the same time the official apologetics of the Russian leadership and its acolytes outside the Soviet Union, including those in Czechoslovakia itself, which were calculated to assist in the process of containing and rolling back the gains which had been made by the working people in the "Czech Spring".

Today, systematic pressure has eroded those gains to a desperately low level. While Mr Michael Stewart has orated about "Western defence" he has intensified the pressures upon the Czechoslovak people, since his whole military system is directed no less at they themselves than at their Soviet and Eastern European occupiers: as often happens, the power structures of West and East have converged to choke out any threat to the status quo. The pressures from the Government of the Soviet Union have been relentless. With the fall of the Dubcek administration, the press was muzzled, the old policemen of Novotny were allowed to creep back into positions of great authority and influence, trade union independence was greatly sapped, and Mr Husak was paraded at a convention of the world's communist parties in order to say that the occupation of his country was "an internal matter" which was no business of anyone else.

But it *is* our business. No socialist can behave as if this invasion has never happened. Not only has the Soviet Government issued a public declaration that it has the right to do the same thing again whenever and wherever it adjudges a need: but even if there were, as there are manifestly not, all the elements of repentance in the politbureau in Moscow, it would still be necessary to address the question of how such military adventures could possibly come about. This question needs answering not only at the level of micro-documentation: it also requires discussion at the level of broad sociological generalisation. This discussion has scarcely begun in the official Marxist parties. True, a number of notions have been canvassed as possible explanations as to how the conflict could have originated. The official Warsaw Pact view is, of course, that counter-revolution was imminent in Prague, and that in the given circumstances it was expedient to declare "a fig for Engels' bourgeois scruples!" and rush to restore whatever was salvable of the blessings of the old Novotny order. This view is shared by Fidel Castro, who believes nonetheless that the action of the Warsaw Pact powers was totally illegal, although "necessary". The Czechs had been busy restoring capitalism, emulating the Yugoslavs, who have already, on this view, restored it. The Chinese and Albanian communists are also all too ready to believe that Mr Dubcek was about to "restore capitalism", but, logically within the confines of such a view, hasten to add that the Russians had already beaten him to it. Between such contending capitalisms, the Czechs have their support, because the Russians are seen as predators and hegemonists.

What sense are we to make of this conflicting mesh of diagnoses? No factories have been auctioned off in any of these countries. The predominant sector of their productive industry remains in public ownership. Czechoslovakia, indeed, had a higher than usual proportion of socialised production. None of them, neither the Czechs, nor the Russians, nor the Warsaw Pact powers in general, have licensed the unlimited freedom of private investment, introduced limited liability companies or anything of the kind. Even in Yugoslavia where the market has more sway than in any other socialised state economy, the basis of public ownership remains generally secure. Can capitalism be restored without capitalists?

Such charges are clearly ideological rather than scientific. They illuminate nothing. What, then, is the social condition of these nations?

The countries we call "socialist" are indeed socialist in one respect in which they have passed beyond the capitalist form of organisation. To be a little more precise, what they have socialised is the means of production. That is to say that private property has either ceased to exist or largely ceased to exist in productive enterprises. It is unnecessary to enter into the argument about what happens when the means of production are undemocratically controlled, although it is perfectly plain that there are, to a very considerable extent, different social and economic laws governing economies which have abrogated the private ownership of property in the means of production to those which apply in an economy which is subject to the dominance of private ownership. That is the first point.

The second point is that none of the socialist countries has yet progressed to the realisation of socialism in the second sense in which the word is understood, which concerns the socialisation of the means of consumption. None of the socialist countries has entered a phase of general welfare distribution of commodities. It is perfectly plain that in the traditional Marxist sense socialism was about socialisation of both the means of production and distribution. It will be said that this insistence mixes up two stages of development: the "socialist" stage, and the "communist" stage which must be seen separately. But there is indeed considerable internal evidence in Marx's writing that by the word "communism" he means a *third* stage which is higher, again, than the second phase of socialisation of distribution, in which money ceased to play a vital role in determining transactions between persons. This third stage involves precisely the ultimate goal of the overcoming of the division of labour itself, as a result of which "we shall hunt in the morning, fish in the afternoon and critically criticise in the evening".

It seems very clear that it is possible to conceive of the abolition of money as a basic relationship between individual people, considerably before it becomes technically possible to evolve an integrated human kind embodying the annulment of the division of labour. If this is taken to be the case, we must be very careful when we apply the word "socialist" to existing communist controlled states. Such countries are socialist in one sense, not yet socialist in another sense. They are socialist in the sense that in most of them the overwhelming majority of the means of production have entered into social ownership. They are non-socialist to the extent that these means of production are by no means ready to support truly social forms of distribution, or where they are ready, are, by various impediments, held back from this necessary development.

This is the problem Fidel Castro was attempting to face, when he spoke, in Cuba, of "building up socialism and communism at the same time".

However, if one can accept a framework of analysis in which the extended evolutionary process toward socialism can be grasped without eschatology, it becomes clear that within each stage of social organisation there can be located various types of structural obstacles to development, and various interests and impulses towards it. These require the attention of socialists all over the world, because in the struggle between them, the model of socialism itself will be marked out.

But the precondition for realistic analysis of this shifting movement is the development of precisely those democratic norms which have been nurtured in the Prague Spring. Without such widespread freedoms, recognised and engrained within the social structure, none of the issues emerge plainly; none of the obstacles are clearly identified.

The repression in Czechoslovakia is therefore a bigger blow to socialism than any imaginable act or proposal of the Dubcek team.

Chapter 4

Dictatorship, Ancient and Modern

Edward Bernstein is dead. So is Karl Kautsky. So, too, are Marx, Engels, Lenin, Trotsky and, happily, Stalin. It is several decades since any social-democrat paid serious attention to the thoughts of either Bernstein or Kautsky, and if either of these pioneers were to return in new incarnations to modern social-democratic Germany they might well find themselves coming under the stigma of the *berufsverbote*. Likewise, it is a considerable time since communist practice even appeared to follow the teachings of the other masters, and General Grigorenko was in fact detained for some years in a Soviet psychiatric prison for believing too literally in Lenin's *State and Revolution*.

All the more remarkable then is the upsurge of interest in the dictatorship of the proletariat, the discussion on which is currently echoing around West European Communist Parties, as the French ceremonially repudiate the concept, while the Italians, close always to the papal court, transubstantiate it into an aetherial notion of hegemony. Now, as a result of all these verbal acrobatics, New Left Books are offering us the dissident French orthodoxy of Etienne Balibar to explain why not a line of Lenin's work is for half a second dispensable*. For a moment, I thought the imprint had changed, as my mind's eye insisted on reading, instead of NLB, Very Old Indeed Left Books.

Let us get six things straight: One: Marx and Engels taken together used the phrase 'dictatorship of the proletariat' altogether sixteen times in eleven distinct writings, all of which cluster into three very narrow periods. Meantime, they wrote six or seven million other words.

Two: in Victorian times, the word 'dictatorship' applied to the classical model of a temporally limited, provisional ad-

*On the Dictatorship of the Proletariat. Etienne Balibar. New Left Books. 1977.

ministration. The most commonly cited example of a dictator was the Roman, Sulla. Careful examination of the Marx usage of the term shows that he thought of it in terms of a revolutionary democratic provisional government, which could in a brief time establish the main socio-political conditions in which communist relations might begin to develop. From the beginning, he associated the notion with the widest democratic participation, the abolition of standing armies and professional police, and the rapid beginning of the 'withering away' of the State.

Three: Lenin, who said communism was "Soviets plus electrification", saw this transition in Russia as possibly taking a bit longer than ten or twenty years (Collected Works, 31, pp 16-7). No-one can read *The State and Revolution* without being aware that Lenin's state would have been expected to be well on the wither by that time.

Four: for all that, Lenin gave an indefensible picture of dictatorship when he said that it was "unrestricted" power, "not restricted in any way, not by any laws, absolutely not constrained by any rules and regulations". Nowhere did Marx hint at such an approach, and, indeed, he frequently insisted that the proletariat was qualified to rule only insofar as it was the sole force whose freedom could bring about the liberation of the whole of society. It is, further, logically quite impossible for a *whole* social class to rule with 'unrestricted' powers, 'absolutely not constrained', because its own rule must inevitably be nullified if it does not quickly evolve rules and regulations, constraints and restrictions which institutionalise its power, embody its concepts of right and justice, and separate its own controlling bodies into rationally accountable powers.

Five: uncountable numbers of dead people bear mute witness to the fact that the 'transition' envisaged by Lenin did not take place. To this day it has not taken place. The new Soviet Constitution is no less the map of a repressive State apparatus than was the old one. It would take a fool to argue that the powers of alleged 'socialist' States were further eroded than those of undoubted 'capitalist' ones. All the modern States are concentrating authority and force to a frightening degree, but the internal repressive mechanisms of the USSR and Eastern Europe are even more developed than those of the USA or Great Britain. If a Freedom of Information Act has unlocked some of the archives of the CIA and FBI, it seems likely that it could be quite a long while before a similar reform will blow a liberal wind through the corridors of the KGB. (And, I fear, maybe, before those who put Agee and Hosenball out of England will have to answer for their decisions).

Six: for all these reasons, it must be highly questionable whether we should continue to accept a distinction between the 'sociological' concept of proletarian dictatorship and its alleged embodiment in 'political' forms. Something went considerably wrong with a 'sociology' which failed to meet its own predictions on so large and drastic a scale.

For six good reasons, then, we are bound to conclude that Balibar offers us a short, well-argued, clear guide to an imaginary fossil-kingdom, a veritable Silmarillion of the Left. On the real planet Earth, however, no States are withering, so no proletarian dictatorships are functioning according to any conceivable variant of the model.

If Tony Crosland's ghost is smiling as he reads these words, it can stop at once. Though Lenin's dream didn't come true, neither in the least did Kautsky's, nor yet has Crosland's, which falsified itself in a far shorter timespan than the others. A long while ago now, a lot of people began to see this, and that was why we started the New Left.

Perhaps we now need a New New Left, to remind people of what we meant then.

Chapter 5

The Separation of Powers

In 1919 Bukharin and Preobrazhensky published a primer for communists which was quickly translated into all the major European languages. *The ABC of Communism* reflected their expectations about the immediate future of Soviet power. On the question of 'proletarian justice', for instance, they wrote:

"As far as the revolutionary tribunals are concerned, this form of proletarian justice has no significance for future days, any more than the Red Army will have any significance for the future after it has conquered the White Guards, or any more than the Extraordinary Commissions have any significance for the future. In a word, all the instruments created by the proletariat for the critical period of the civil war are transient. When the counter-revolution has been successfully crushed, these instruments will no longer be needed, and they will disappear.

"On the other hand, proletarian justice in the form of the elective popular courts will unquestionably survive the end of the civil war, and will for a long period have to continue the use of measures to deal with the vestiges of bourgeois society in its manifold manifestations. The abolition of classes will not result in the immediate abolition of class ideology, which is more long-lived than are the social conditions which have produced it, more enduring than the class instincts and class customs which have brought it into being. Besides, the abolition of class may prove a lengthy process. The transformation of the bourgeoisie into working folk and that of the peasants into the workers of a socialist society will be a tardy affair. The change in peasant ideology is likely to be very slow, and will give plenty of work to the law-courts. Moreover, during the period which must precede the full development of communist distribution, the period during which the articles of consumption are still privately owned, there will be ample occasion for delinquencies and crimes. Finally, anti-social offences arising out of personal egoism, and all sorts of offences against the common weal, will long continue to provide work for the courts. It is true that these courts will gradually change in character. As the State dies out, they will tend to become simply organs for the expression of public opinion. They will assume the character of courts of arbitration. Their decisions will no longer be enforced by physical means and will have a purely moral significance."*

One does not need to follow Solzhenitsyn's account of the origins of the *Gulag Archipelago* to know that Bukharin's hopes

*University of Michigan, Ann Arbor, 1966, pp 225-6.

were not fulfilled. When Bukharin himself was shot, shortly after playing a major role in the drafting of the 'most democratic constitution in the world' nothing could more powerfully highlight the advantage in simple terms of civil and personal liberty, of bourgeois right as represented in the 'bourgeois doctrine of the separation of powers'* Almost every independent socialist thinker of the generation which has matured since 1956 has understood this simple truth, and that is why very few can be persuaded of the divine inspiration of such scriptures as *The State and Revolution,* which argues deliberately for the notion of a coalescence of legislative and executive functions. This might be an appropriate doctrine had the division of labour been finally overcome, but it is not a very acceptable one in the real, material and evolvingly wicked world. Of course legislative and executive functions can be separated in different ways: they can be divided in order to neutralise the power of legislators, or in order to control the activities of professional administrators. They can also be separated in order to minimise accountability or in order to maximise it.

Many of the more utopian neo-Leninist socialists seem to regard the separation of powers as simply itself an extension of the division of labour, and therefore retrogressive. The truth is the exact contrary: any democratic form in which the separation functions effectively will discover in it a powerful weapon against the atrophy of roles, and a constant stimulus to the erosion of particularised power-centres and fortified in-group interests.** So elementary is this truth that every workers' organisation applies it almost automatically. The simplest working men's clubs or associations elect a secretary, and then pace him with a separate treasurer whose job it is to stop him spending all the money, whereupon they immediately appoint separate auditors to control any lack of due public spirit in the conservation of the funds. Once an organisation is so clique ridden that one caucus can determine the occupancy of all these offices without challenge, it is in danger, be it never so revolutionary. The same is true in the domain of a bourgeois state

* See Stephen F. Cohen's important biography: *Bukharin and the Bolshevik Revolution,* Wildwood House, 1974.
** Cf. in this connection, the most important treatment by Mihailo Markovic, in *On the Legal Institutions of Socialist Democracy,* Spokesman Pamphlets, 1976.

which has separated the judiciary from the executive, (often imperfectly at that), and then, after dividing the executive from the legislature, loudly cried halt.

The struggle for democracy in fact deploys a wide arsenal of weapons, starting with direct elections and strong accountability, but including a wide variety of controls over the use of power, which can include many relevant checks and balances not to be found described in classic doctrine.

That is why any transitional society which learns from Bukharin's fate will go far beyond the bourgeoisie in insisting on this crucial principle. This is also why any statutory party monopoly of authority is an abomination, for even if there is a juridical separation between executive and judiciary, if one caucus nominates both lists, justice will always be in danger. Bukharin's and Lenin's dream of the withering away of the State, and the overcoming of punishment by proletarian morality, might, or might not, have been a plausible short-term target if the judges in the USSR were even as imperfectly adjusted to humanist notions of penology as the vegetarian fringes of the modern English magistracy: but it was just not seriously possible with the Party in effective control of the 'elections' for the judiciary. I doubt whether there is a single Russian judge today who doesn't think that both Bukharin and Lenin were completely mistaken about matters of crime and punishment. If I am seriously wrong, then there is sufficient genuine schizophrenia on the modern Russian bench to keep Soviet psychiatry honourably engaged for many happy years after it has been relieved of the problem of eliminating untoward opinions.

All this reasoning was much to be heard in the arguments which took place after the 20th Congress of the CPSU. It burst into life again in the Action Programme of the Czechoslovak Communist Party:

> "The communists in the government, too, must ensure as soon as possible that the principle of responsibility of the government towards the National Assembly covering all its activities is worked out in detail. Even under the existing practice of political management, the opportunity afforded for independent activity of the government and of individual ministers was not sufficiently made use of, there was a tendency to shift responsibility onto the Party bodies and to evade independence in decision taking. The government is not only an organ of economic policy. As the supreme executive organ of the State it must, as a whole, deal systematically with the whole scope of political and administrative problems of the State. It is also up to the government to take care of the rational development of the whole State machinery.

The State administration machinery was often underrated in the past; this machinery must consist of highly qualified people, professionally competent and rationally organised, it must be subject to a systematic supervision in a democratic way, it must be effective. Simplified ideas as if such goals could be attained by underrating and decrying the administrative machinery in general were rather detrimental in the past.

"In the whole State and political system it is necessary to create, purposefully, such relations and rules that would, on the one hand, provide the necessary safeguards to professional officials in their functions and, on the other hand, enable the necessary replacement of officials who can no longer cope with their work by professionally and politically more competent people. This means to establish legal conditions for the recall of responsible officials and to provide legal guarantees of decent conditions for those who are leaving their posts through the normal way of replacement, so that their departure should not amount to a 'drop' in their material and moral political standing.

"The Party policy is based on the principle that no undue concentration of power must occur, throughout the State machinery, in one sector, one body, or in a single individual. It is necessary to provide for such a division of power and such a system of mutual supervision that any faults or encroachments of any of its links are rectified in time, by the activities of another link. This principle must be applied, not only to relations between the elected and executive bodies, but also to the inner relations of the State administration machinery and to the standing and activities of courts of law.

"This principle is infringed mainly by undue concentration of duties in the existing ministry of the interior. The Party thinks it necessary to make of it a ministry for internal State security. The schedule that in our State was traditionally within the jurisdiction of other bodies and with the passage of time has been incorporated into the ministry of the interior, must be withdrawn from it. It is necessary to elaborate proposals as soon as possible passing on the main responsibility for investigation to the courts of law, separating prison administration from the security force, and handling over press law administration, of archives, etc., to other State bodies.

"The Party considers the problem of a correct incorporation of the security force in the State as politically very important. The security of our lives will only benefit, if everything is eliminated that helps to maintain a public view of the security force marred by the past period of law violations and by the privileged position of the security force in the political system. That past period impaired the progressive traditions of our security force as a force advancing side-by-side with our people. These traditions must be renewed. The Central Committee of the Communist Party of Czechoslovakia deems it necessary to change the organisation of the security force and to split the joint organisation into two mutually independent parts — State Security and Public Security. The State Security service must have such a status, organisational structure, numerical state, equipment, methods of work, and qualifications which are in keeping with its work of defending the State from the activities of enemy centres abroad. Every citizen who has not been culpable in this respect must know with certainty that his political convictions and opinions, his personal beliefs and activities, cannot be the object of attention of the bodies of the State Security Service. The Party declares clearly that this apparatus should not be directed and used to solve internal political questions and controversies in socialist society.

"The Public Security Service will fulfil tasks in combating crime and in the protection of public order; for this its organisation, numerical state and methods of work must be adapted. The Public Security Force must be better equipped and strengthened; its functions in the defence of public order must be exactly laid down by law and, in their fulfilment, the service will be directed by the national committees. Legal norms must create clearer relations of control over the security force by the government as a whole and by the National Assembly.

It is necessary to devote the appropriate care to carrying out the defence policy in our State. In this connection it is necessary to work for our active share in the conception of the military doctrine of the Warsaw Treaty countries, the strengthening of the defence potential of our country in harmony with its needs and possibilities, a uniform complex understanding of the questions of defence with all problems of the building of socialism in the whole of our policy, including defence training.

"The legal policy of the Party is based on the principle that in a dispute over right — including adminstrative decisions of State bodies — the basic guarantee of legality is proceedings in court which are independent of political factors and are bound only by law. The application of this principle requires a strengthening of the whole social and political role and importance of courts of law in our society. The Central Committee of the Communist Party of Czechoslovakia will see to it that work on the complex of the required proposals and measures proceeds so as to find the answer to all the necessary problems before the next election of judges. In harmony with and parallel to that, it is also necessary to solve the status and duties of the public prosecutor's office so that it may not be put above the courts of law, and to guarantee full independence of barristers and solicitors from State bodies."*

How was this argument received in the other Warsaw Pact powers? Walter Ulbricht gave a consensual view in his statement at the 20th anniversary of the founding of the Walter Ulbricht Academy of Political Science and Law on 12 October 1968:

"Socialist democracy has nothing in common with the bourgeois 'separation of powers' or with 'separation and control of power'. In the struggle of the working class for the establishment of its political power we have taken issue with the theory of the separation of powers not only once. This question was already on the agenda during the November Revolution. Also the Weimar Constitution proclaimed the separation of powers and even declared it to be a typical example of a parliamentary democracy, in which 'the relations of the legislative, executive and judicial organs' should be based on their reciprocal independence and reciprocal control. But this so-called separation of powers really means nothing but the limitation of the rights of parliament and the guarantee of the class-biased independent activity of the majority of the civil servants and masters of justice educated by the bourgeoisie. The Social Democratic Party (SPD) was in government power for a long time in the Weimar Republic. But the result was not 'democratic socialism', but undivided imperialist dictatorship, and the final result was fascism. Today West German imperialism marshalls its State monopoly rule in alliance with American imperialism and also calls it 'marshalled rule'. This new phase of State development is characterised by the emergency laws, the 'internal State reform', 'territorial and administrative reform', the 'concerted action' of

* *The Action Programme of the Czechoslovak Communist Party,* Spokesman Pamphlet, No.8, p.12.

Messrs Strauss and Schiller, the demands for strengthening and consolidating NATO and the concentration of the rule of the most aggressive forces of imperialism. There is not the least trace of a separation of power. Solely the decorative elements of certain plenary and committee meetings are left.

"The slogan of the 'separation of powers' is kept handy for the socialist countries, however. But with whom are the working people to divide power? Are they to divide power with the gentlemen in Bonn, the neo-nazis and Hitler generals or with the adherents of the forces of the exploiting classes deprived of their power, like those who crept out of their holes in Czechoslovakia and organised themselves in the various clubs in order to annul the achievements of socialism and restore the old conditions? This twaddle about the separation of powers originates from the veiled counter-revolution and is part of the programme of the global strategy of imperialism.

"We have drawn the lessons from the history of class struggle that only one real guarantee of democracy exists: the working people must eliminate this system of bourgeois class rule inimical to the people, its basis of power in the economy under the leadership of the unitedly acting working class and take political and economic power into their own hands and set up their own democratic State. This State can only be constructed on the foundation of the concentration of power in the hands of the elected people's representatives and their close active relationship with the working people and their collectives. The democratic management of all administrative organs of the State and of justice is effected on the basis of this sovereignty of the people. That is also the reason why there is no room in our State order for administrative courts. These administrative courts existing in capitalist countries are only to replace the activity of parliamentary committees and increase the power of reactionary administrative officials."*

In the juxtaposition of these two views, we see a conflict which divides the entire Socialist Movement, without respect for agreement which may subsist on other issues. Reformist or revolutionary, 'parliamentary' or 'Soviet', every group of socialists includes those whose instinct is to concentrate powers in the hands of the good and the just, and those whose instinct is to adapt institutions so as to prevent the abuse of power.

Of course, Ulbricht is quite justified in claiming that by itself the disembodied doctrine of separation of powers has no positive leverage for social transformation. Indeed the doctrine as such will not even prevent injustice, which can only be thwarted when living and active men are prepared to make use of all the powers they have, and invent such new powers as they need, in defence of a cause. If one looks back at the Czechoslovaks' *Action Programme* one sees that the Dubcek team wished to extend the doctrine of separation of powers to the development of cadres policy. This innovation would

* Walter Ulbricht: *The Role of the Socialist State in the Shaping of the Developed Social System of socialism,* Verlag Zeit Im Bild, Berlin, DDR, 1968.

foreshadow many others. Was it not a form of separation of powers which uncovered the Watergate conspiracy in the United States? Is not the separation of the press from centralised control indispensable to a free society? Cannot the East German leaders recollect the impassioned appeals of the young Karl Marx for freedom from censorship? Is there nowadays some sinister theoretical principle which sanctifies proletarian censorship, while condemning all other forms? A careful reading of Marx would clearly establish that in his time *he* did not think so.

Ulbricht makes a convincing case that the doctrine of separation of powers has not undermined the bourgeois order, either in Germany or elsewhere. Why then should it undermine a proletarian order? Is Ulbricht telling us that proletarian rule is incompatible with any autonomous idea of justice? We invariably receive a similar type of response when leaders of established communist governments are asked why a genuine plurality of working class political parties cannot be allowed to contend within a socialist constitutional framework. Then we are always told that parties represent social classes, and that, since the communist party has pre-empted working class representation, none other may exist without opening restorationist prospects. Yet, bourgeois States may secrete a diverse collection of parties, giving expression to an enormous variety of interests, all of which remain completely bourgeois. Is the working class less sociologically complex than the bourgeoisie? The notion is absurd. Once one admits, however, that this complexity exists, one immediately confronts a need for pluralistic forms of representation of shifting patterns of interest: and the associated need for transitional *socialist* forms of separation of powers.

Chapter 6

Remembering Khodzhayev
(and others)

I

Not many Western readers take out subscriptions to *Sharq yulduzi* which has a circulation of 167,000 in Soviet Bukhara. *Star of the East* as we would know it, is published in Tashkent, where it is the Uzbek language literary monthly, and in 1978 it ran a celebratory feature on Faizulla Khodzhayev, which not many Western readers ran out to procure:

> "Those who have fought for the people's happiness are never forgotten", said this article, "They are preserved eternally in the people's memory, and pass from generation to generation."*

Such memories were provoked by a picture-book, issued in Tashkent in 1977. This work is named after its subject, the same Faizulla Khodzhayev, who is pictured on the cover in his military uniform: which provokes an explanation. "Some readers", says the reviewer, "are not well aware that he (Khodzhayev) was the first General to emerge from the Uzbeks, or that he attained the highest military rank of those times". However, Soviet President Brezhnev is aware, and indeed he is cited:

> "those who were nurtured by the Party of Lenin, Akmad Ikramov, Faizulla Khodzhayev . . . and many other comrades are remembered by us today with gratitude and respect."**

With such patronage, it is not altogether surprising that *Sharq yulduzi* can culminate its appreciation of the first Uzbek general by announcing that he "was a true son of the people".

Things were not always like that. Forty years earlier, the Uzbek press had been less flattering about him, but then Khodzhayev was very much better known in the West.

---

*   I am indebted to Professor Stephen Cohen and Mr James Crichlow for this information, monitored by Mr Crichlow.

** From a speech of 24 September 1973.

On 2 March 1938 he appeared before the military collegium of the supreme court of the USSR, charged alongside 20 other defendants with "having, on the instructions of intelligence services of foreign States" instigated acts of espionage, diversonism, terrorism, and several other major crimes. Khodzhayev was sentenced to death, and executed immediately after the trial. Alongside him were shot the other major victims of the same process, former prime minister A.I. Rykov, and internationally known communist leader, N.I. Bukharin. The show trial which produced this result was the concluding act in a long drama, following earlier trials in which nearly all the former leaders of the Russian Revolution were 'proved' to have betrayed it from its earliest years and before.*

At the Bukharin trial, Khodzhayev confessed to plotting with the former head of the Communist International in order to convert Uzbekistan and Turkmenia into British protectorates. He also confessed to meeting Bukharin in 1936 and discussing an agreement with fascist Germany (which Bukharin denied) and overtures to Japan (which Bukharin also denied). The verdict of the court was that Khodzhayev himself and Ikramov (who was also, in 1978, remembered by Mr Brezhnev "with gratitude and respect") had:

> "developed extensive diversive (sic) and wrecking activities . . . in Uzbekistan with the object of causing discontent among the population and thus creating favourable conditions for the preparations of armed actions against the Soviet power at the time of foreign intervention."

It was for this reason that both men were immediately despatched by bullets, after suffering "the confiscation of all their personal property".

Of the 21 defendants at the Bukharin trial, all but three were executed. Seven of those killed were subsequently posthumously rehabilitated. Besides Khodzhayev and Ikramov, Krestinsky, Ivanov, Chernov, Grinko and Zelensky were all, during the years between 1956 and 1964, declared to have been innocent. Any dependents who survived them were thus rendered eligible for the pension rights and other emoluments due to the survivors of senior political leaders. But while the exoneration of a full third of the trial cast list leaves the remaining trial record totally without credibility, even totally without rudimentary logic, the

* I have made a documentary report on this case, in the light of some modern evidence, in *The Case of Nikolai Bukharin,* Spokesman, 1978.

juridical process as a whole has never been revised by the Soviet courts.

At the same time that the Tashkent publishing house was proofing its picture book on the first Uzbek general, Bukharin's family was, according to a widely circulated samizdat document,* receiving a somewhat dustier answer from authority:

"Early in June 1977, an official of the Central Committee, Klimov, phoned at the apartment of A.M. Larina (N.I. Bukharin's widow) and asked that she get in touch with him. On June 9, since A.M. Larina was out of Moscow, Yu. N. Larin, her son and son of N.I. Bukharin, called the number indicated by Klimov and asked him hadn't he phoned in connection with the letters sent by Bukharin's son and widow on the eve of the 25th Congress (of the Communist Party of the Soviet Union) to the Congress itself, to the Presidium of the Congress, to the Politburo of the Central Committee of the Communist Party of the Soviet Union, and personally to the General Secretary of the Central Committee, CPSU, L.I. Brezhnev, appealing for Bukharin's rehabilitation. Klimov confirmed that his call was connected with this matter and said the following:

"I have been instructed to inform you that your appeal to have Bukharin reinstated in the Party and restored to full membership in the Academy of Sciences of the USSR cannot be granted since the guilty verdicts pertaining to the criminal offences for which he was tried have not been set aside."

Yu. N. Larin replied that many of Bukharin's co-defendant's had been rehabilitated; for example, Krestinsky, Ikramov and Khodzhayev.

Klimov answered that obviously Larin didn't know that the majority of the accused at the trial had not been rehabilitated.

Yu. N. Larin asked, "Do you really believe that Nikolai Ivanovich (Bukharin) murdered Gorky?"

Klimov answered, "That question falls under the jurisdiction of the courts and the procurator's office."

Yu. N. Larin asked, "Does that mean that you think I should turn to these bodies?"

To this Klimov answered: "That's your right," but made it clear he oughtn't to do that at the present time. "You should know how complicated the situation is now."

A.M. Larina and Yu. N. Larin first appealed for N.I. Bukharin's rehabilitation in 1961. Thus the rejection came 16 years after the first request and a year-and-a-half after the last. (V.I. Lenin's friends, E.D. Stasova and V.A. Karpinsky, having made an analogous appeal in 1965, died and consequently never got an answer).

Having received the foregoing statement, Yu. N. Larin addressed a petition for Bukharin's rehabilitation to the Chairman of the Supreme Court of the USSR on 11 June 1977."

Whether or not this remarkably obtuse reaction can be explained by a hankering to forgive Stalin on the part of some sec-

---

* Cf. *In These Times*, 16-22 November 1977, p.13.

tion of the Central Committee of the CPSU, it is tragically plain that Larin and his mother have, since 11 June 1977, got precisely nowhere in their efforts to secure belated justice for Bukharin.

This explains why, the following year, while the *Star of the East* was honouring Khodzhayev, Larin seized upon the anniversary of the death of his father to appeal to Enrico Berlinguer, the general secretary of the Communist Party of Italy, for help. In an extraordinary letter, which brings the bygone atmosphere of the late 'thirties manacingly back to life, he wrote:

Respected Comrade Berlinguer,

I am writing this letter to you on the eve of the 40th Anniversary of the tragic death of my father, Nikolai Ivanovich Bukharin. At that time I was only two years old and naturally was unable to remember my father. But my mother, who had spent many years in Stalin's prisons and camps, miraculously survived and told me the truth about my father. Later G.M. Krzhizhanovsky, one of V.I. Lenin's closest friends, and Old Bolsheviks, who had lived through the terror and who had known Nikolai Ivanovich in one circumstance or another, told me about him. In addition I read many Bolshevist books (which are banned in our country even today, and have been preserved only by chance by certain old Bolsheviks) including books by Nikolai Ivanovich himself, and the works of foreign researchers. The information which I obtained in this way helped me to fully appreciate the character and the social and political activity of my father. I understood the enormity of Stalin's crimes, the extent to which he had falsified the history of the Party, the absurdity and stupidity of the accusations levelled against my father at the Plenum of the Central Committee of February/March 1937 and the trial of the so-called 'Right-Trotskyist Bloc'. However, on the basis of these absurd charges (espionage, treason, sabotage and murder), my father was expelled from the Central Committee and from the Party and condemned to death.

Beginning in 1961, my mother A.M. Larina and then I myself, persistently raised with the highest Party/State organs of the country the question of the withdrawal of the monstrous allegations against N.I. Bukharin and his restoration to Party membership. This question was also raised with the Party leadership by the most senior of the Old Bolsheviks led by the former secretary of the Central Committee of the Party, E.D. Staseva. They died some time ago without receiving an answer and it was only last summer (1977) that we at last received some response in the form of a telephone call. An official of the Commission of Party Control of the Central Committee of the CPSU informed us by telephone that the accusations made at the trial of Bukharin had not been withdrawn as the process of examining the documents relating to the trial had not been completed; the question of the restoration of his Party membership could not, therefore, yet be resolved. This means that 40 years after the execution of my father we have received an answer, which, in effect, confirms the monstrous charges of Stalin. My approach to the Courts (the Supreme Court of the USSR) has been fruitless: the simple truth is they don't answer me.

In a country where the greater part of the population has been brought up on the mendacious 'Short Course' there are many who still consider my father as a traitor and a hireling of Hitler, although in reality the truth is that he was an outstanding fighter against fascism and in his last years he devoted all his energies to the exposure of fascism and to warnings against the growing fascist threat.

Leaving home for the last time for the Plenum of February/March 1937 (from which he never returned) my father said to my mother, "don't become embittered: there are sad errors in history. I want my son to grow up as a Bolshevik". He looked on the events which had occurred as tragic but transient; he believed in the ultimate victory of the forces of socialism.

I am not a member of the Party but for my father the word 'Bolshevik' undoubtedly meant a fighter for social justice. And we are unable to obtain such justice in our country for a man whom Lenin, before his death, called "the favourite of the whole Party". For my mother, who lived through the horrors of Stalin's camps, who knew many of Lenin's comrades-in-arms, representatives of the old Bolshevik Party — people about whom she preserves in her memory the happiest recollections and of whom she always speaks with tenderness and love — life in such a situation is becoming more and more intolerable. It is inconceivable that people who still carry on their shoulders the burden of Stalin's crimes and have not cast it into the dustbin of history can fight for high ideals.

I am approaching you, Comrade Berlinguer, not only because you are the leader of the largest Communist Party of Western Europe and have thrown off this burden, but also because N.I. Bukharin was a Communist Internationalist, an active member of the International Workers' Movement. He was known to Communists of many countries; they always recalled him with warmth. Some of them are still living and are working in the ranks of the Italian Communist Party. I particularly have in mind Comrade Umberto Terracini.

I am approaching you to ask you to participate in the campaign for the rehabilitation of my father, in whatever form seems to you to be most appropriate.

Not long before his death Nikolai Ivanovich wrote a letter "to the future generation of leaders of the Party" in which he appealed to them "to unravel the monstrous 'tangle of crimes' ". My mother learnt the text of this letter by heart in the dark days and after her rehabilitation she passed it on to the Central Committee of the Party. This letter ended with the words:

"Know comrades that on the banner which you will carry in your victorious march towards Communism there is a drop of my blood."

Yours sincerely,

12.3.78   Yu. Larin (Bukharin)

This message was communicated to the Russell Foundation, which circulated it in many countries for endorsement, and secured a very wide response.

First, from the Italian Communists, the distinguished Party historian, Paolo Spriano, was quickly joined by other Party leaders in endorsing an appeal to President Brezhnev for action on the Larin letter. Then, within a few weeks, other Euro-Communist spokesmen also joined in: first the Spanish, then the Belgians, then the British. Soon the Australian Communists added their voices. Socialist and Labour Parties in England, France, Austria and Italy followed on. By November 1978 the

French Communist Party had published its appeal for the rehabilitation of Bukharin, and virtually all the major left-wing parties of Europe were united in urging that the Soviet authorities respond to the poignant appeal of Bukharin's family.

II

After the Russell Foundation had circulated Larin's appeal to Berlinguer I wrote a little book on the Bukharin case. In the course of preparing this I came across an interesting statement by N.S. Khrushchev published in the first volume of his memoirs. He said that just before the Twentieth Party Congress in 1956 he was told by Rudenko that, "from the standpoint of judicial norms, there was no evidence whatsoever for condemning or even trying those men. The case for prosecuting them had been based on personal confessions beaten out of them under physical and psychological torture, and confessions extracted by such means are unacceptable as legitimate basis for bringing someone to trial".

However nothing was said about the trials because, "there had been representatives of the fraternal Communist parties present when Rykov, Bukharin, and other leaders of the people were tried and sentenced. These representatives had then gone home and testified in their own countries to the justice of the sentences. We didn't want to discredit the fraternal Party representatives who had attended the open trials, so we indefinitely postponed the rehabilitation of Bukharin, Zinoviev, Rykov and the rest".

Khrushchev's memory was, of course, very selective and sometimes downright wrong: so much so that western scholars did not believe that the first volume of these recollections could be genuine. However, prior to the publication of the second volume, the publishers made available to independent investigators the tapes from which the memoirs were compiled. There can be no doubt, therefore, that Khrushchev actually said that the rehabilitation of Bukharin was under consideration at an early stage in the preparation of the 20th Congress.

I sent the proofs of my tract on the Bukharin case to Zhores Medvedev, the exiled Soviet bio-chemist. He was interested in Khrushchev's statement, and in a letter he threw a further light on the question. Following a visit to the theatre in 1968 to see a play called "Bolsheviks" Khrushchev is reported to have said that Bukharin and Kamenev were among the group of leaders whose rehabilitation was under consideration in 1958.

The resolution about the reconsideration of the Moscow show trials had already been made ready. Arguments from Maurice Thorez of the French Communist Party that, "after the XXth Congress and the Hungarian events we lost almost half of our Party . . . formally to rehabilitate those who were tried in the open trials could lose the rest", influenced the decision not to proceed.

When this information was released to journalists, many of them recollected a contemporary story about Khrushchev's visit to the theatre, although the version which reached the west at that time was not so complete as that given by Dr Medvedev. The English socialist press published his letter in full and this provoked a number of comments. The most important of these concerned Khrushchev's recollection about the membership of the French Communist Party. Of course, the official statistics of that Party's membership do not reveal any such catastrophe as that reported in this letter. Was Khrushchev jumbling up protests made by different Communist leaders? Or had the French Communists been dissembling when they reported their membership statistics in public? A controversy on this matter began, and this provoked a second letter from Dr Medvedev which contained the following passages.

"For the crucial meeting of the Party Presidium at which the Bukharin case was to be discussed, some foreign Communist leaders were invited. Among these were Maurice Thorez and Harry Pollitt.

"At this meeting, 20 rehabilitation cases, including those of Bukharin and his co-defendants, and some other former leaders, were completed for reconsideration. The conclusions of the Supreme Court and the General Prosecutor about the innocence of these persons were distributed to the meeting for its final approval.

"At this meeting, a very strong polemic took place between Thorez and Khrushchev. Khrushchev was in favour of rehabilitation, Thorez against. ("For the sake of the movement.") Khrushchev became angry. He almost lost his temper — "You are not a real Communist if you are afraid of the truth!" he exclaimed. However, Harry Pollitt supported the position taken by Thorez. Probably the immediate rehabilitation of so many prominent victims was not supported by some of the other participants in the meeting: it is clear that Khrushchev did not secure majority support.

"One thing, however, is certain. The legal process of reconsidering the trial had been completed and the innocence of Bukharin, Rykov and others had been established. But the final publication and confirmation of these legal findings did not take place, and the grounds for this had nothing to do with criteria of justice or truth."

The movements of Harry Pollitt as recollected by his biographer, show that Pollitt had been ill during 1956, and had been replaced as General Secretary of his Party by John Gollan. From that time he had become the Party Chairman. But he did spend some time in Moscow during the 40th anniversary of the Soviet Revolution in November 1957. These celebrations took place after the rehabilitation of Tukhachevsky, which seems to have been partially responsible for frictions between Khrushchev and the army leader, Zhukov. Can it be that the meeting in question took place in November 1957? Now that the French Communists are openly discussing their relationship with the Soviet Communists, is it possible that they could open their archives in order to produce some answer to this enigma?

III

As this note is written, two years have passed since the argument came to a head in Europe. Bukharin has been the subject of a scholarly conference at the Gramsci Institute in Rome, a meeting of 1,500 cadres of the Chinese Communist Party have solemnly discussed his legacy (and his innocence) in Peking. But in the USSR all remains as it was: neither innocent nor guilty, Bukharin remains in limbo, where he is not remembered, either with or without 'gratitude and respect'. Yet, as the interest in Bukharin's writings* grows among specialists outside the Soviet Union his message remains one that requires attention. For better or worse, he was a main architect of modern communism, and thus, in unvarnished truth, one of the makers of the 20th century.

* N.I. Bukharin: *Writings on the State and the Transition to Socialism,* Spokesman, 1982.

Chapter 7

The Old Soviet Entertainer

Hardly anyone believed that the first volume of Khrushchev's memories, serialised in *Life* magazine and syndicated in posh newspapers around the 'free world', were anything other than an elaborate con-trick. The professors of Kremlinology, if they wrote about the work at all, tended to speculate about who had invented it: was it written by a posse of CIA dirty-tricksters, or was it a hard-currency fiddle by the KGB?

Khrushchev himself reinforced this scepticism when he issued a statement declaring that the handsomely produced volume which emerged was a fabrication. "The venal bourgeois press", he wrote, "has many times been exposed in such lies."

So it has. But now, it transpires, the venal bourgeois press was, after all, telling the truth.

Stranger than fiction, the former premier of the Soviet Union and first secretary of the CPSU did, in fact, spend his last days recording his memoirs for the foremost periodical publishing house in the imperial metropolis. The tapes exist to prove it.

This remarkable fact alone speaks tellingly about the present political structure of the Soviet Union. Notwithstanding the celebrated secret speech by Khrushchev himself, and not-withstanding the subsequent de-Stalinisation, political decisions are still taken in rooms which are probably no less smoke-filled, and certainly no less securely fortified from public scrutiny, than those other British political cloisters denounced by Tony Benn in the general election campaign.

Not for Nikita Khrushchev the descent into officially approved belles-lettres, so general in bourgeois democracies. Not even a posthumous, and carefully scrutinised, autobiography, could be taken for granted by a former Prime Minister in the Moscow of the early seventies.

Accordingly, the most interesting Russian premier since 1924 has now become two volumes sponsored by an impeccably con-

servative, not to say reactionary, American capitalist publisher.*
If I find this rather disgraceful, it is not because I blame
Khrushchev alone for what is, on any assessment, a monumental
apostasy. Apostates will always be judged against the tenets of
the creeds from which they dissent.

But what kind of Luther is it who defies Rome in order the
more fiercely to protest his loyalty to her decrees? These
memoirs are quite extraordinary in their desire to uphold what
the Soviet establishments regards as 'patriotic' values, and yet
they have been smuggled abroad, during the culminating and
most terrible phase of the Vietnam war — which, we should
recall, embroiled a nation allied to the Soviet Union — and they
have been disseminated far and wide by capitalist newspapers.

When Academician Sakharov releases his urgent pleas for
help for political prisoners, he finds himself the victim of menac-
ing enquiries from the security forces. Yet here is a former
premier passing his own form of *samizdat,* including his own
highly distinctive comment on Soviet diplomacy, not to the
liberal or radical press, but to *Time/Life!* If anything can serve
as a memorial to the state of the free press in the Soviet Union,
this bizarre fact is enough.

The volume is full of earthy saws from the old entertainer.
"With my own ears", he informs us, "I heard Beria say that
Stalin had told him at the beginning of the war 'Everything is
lost. I give up. Lenin left us a proletarian State, and now we've
been caught with our pants down and let the whole thing go to
shit!' "

But it is also full of retrospective judgments on the actions of
the Soviet government which are 'liberal' in the extreme, com-
pared to the actions of the author's successors. In hindsight,
Khrushchev would like to have published *Dr Zhivago,* would
like to have given an exit visa to Kapitza and would now be, if he
could, more tolerant of artistic licence.

It is clear from these pages that Khrushchev did have a genuine desire to get out from under some of the worst inherited
debris of Stalinism, and that, for all his uncouthness, he was far
more civilised than some of the slimier kulturniks of the writers'
union.

British readers who remember Aldermaston, and there are a

* *Khrushchev Remembers: The Last Testament.* Translated and edited by
Strobe Talbot. Andre Deutsch, 1971 & 1974.

few, will find the repentant Khrushchev an extraordinary witness. If only we had then had on public record what is now revealed in the semi-privacy of these papers — about Sakharov's lobby against the testing of H-bombs, about Khrushchev's dismissal of it, and about the Soviet premier's private thoughts — I think that CND would have reached higher, faster and further than even Hugh Gaitskell feared.

"I asked our scientists", muses Khrushchev the memoirist, "where we could use the bomb in case of war. I wanted to have a concrete idea about what destruction of this magnitude really meant. I was told that we wouldn't be able to bomb West Germany with a 57-megaton bomb because the prevailing westerly winds would blow the fall-out over the German Democratic Republic, inficting damage both on the civilian population and our own armed forced stationed there. However, we would not jeopardise ourselves or our allies if we dropped the bomb on England, Spain, France or the United States.

"It was a terrifying weapon. It gave us an opportunity to exert moral pressure on those who were conducting aggressive policies against the Soviet Union."

As against these considerations, which I still find scary (although even so I wonder whether the Pentagon is quite as scrupulous in its estimates of the possible ill-effects on West Germany of any similar bombardment of East Germany?), we have the very brave testimony which Sakharov offered to Khrushchev, now reprinted with a series of statements on civil liberty, democracy and détente.*

Sakharov and Khrushchev are compatriots, who have shared, from different vantage points, in the development of exciting (and terrifying) new events. Each has had a large, if entirely distinctive, role in the hopeful movement towards destalinisation. Each has been involved in the decision to make hydrogen bombs, and each has had to face, in his own way, the moral result of this decision. All this is a complex story indeed.

To make it all the more complex, there is another fact. Many Western socialists will find themselves agreeing with some of the things Khrushchev says, yet disapproving of him; while they may well disagree profoundly with Sakharov, and find him nonetheless an admirable person. Who said the work of social and political analysis was getting easier?

* *Sakharov Speaks.* Andrei D. Sakharov. Collins, 1974.

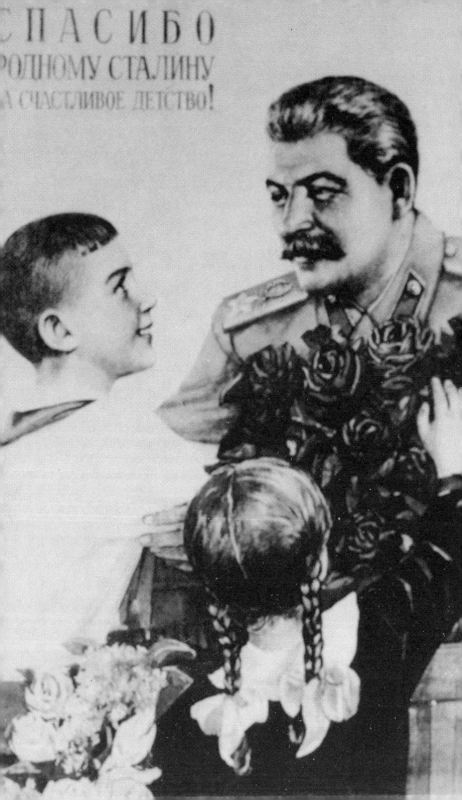

СПАСИБО
РОДНОМУ СТАЛИНУ
ЗА СЧАСТЛИВОЕ ДЕТСТВО!

Chapter 8

Recollections of
Hope and Despair

I

Two birthdays, 100 years ago: October 26 and December 21, 1979 saw the arrival, first of Trotsky, then of Stalin, on a planet in which they were at different times to awaken, among more generous spirits, both great hopes and deep despair.

Now, at the time of their centenary, their homeland marks their memory with conspicuous, almost tangible, silence — perhaps, we might add, fearful silence in the one case, embarrassed silence in the other.

And yet, although publishers outside the Soviet Union continue to issue volume after volume of explanation, rationalisation or apology for one or the other of these fallen giants — and although Western universities convene large seminars and symposia to explore their legacies — nonetheless the most fascinating contribution to the celebration comes from a Russian, having been written in defiance of official displeasure in Moscow, where it has no immediate prospect of being published for its natural audience.

Roy Medvedev's latest work* might with almost equal justice be also subtitled *On Trotsky and Trotskyism*. One of the most interesting differences between this work and the earlier masterly judgment in *Let History Judge*** is that, in the intervening years, Medvedev has been able to study a file of Trotsky's exiled broadsheet, *The Bulletin of the Opposition*.

This is an historic event in its own right, since the handful of contemporary Russian readers of that Bulletin at the moment of its publication were all, virtually without exception, killed. Medvedev is the first modern Soviet scholar to offer his reac-

---

*   *On Stalin and Stalinism* by Roy A. Medvedev. Oxford University Press, 1979.
**   Let History Judge by Roy A. Medvedev. Spoksesman, 1976.

tions to this archive, and this fact gives his book an importance that changes history in a very direct sense. Honest and informed discussion of the overall political evolution of the Soviet Union has hitherto been quite impossible in that country, since numerous key participants who perished in the course of that development have, at the same moment, been erased from memory by the censorship.

Stalin does not emerge from these remarkable pages with any greater credit than he had earned in *Let History Judge*. Medvedev has tracked down and catalogued a lot more murders, and has arrived at more accurate tallies of the death roll, which he states baldly, without hyperbole, and without the exaggerations of such other writers as Solzhenitsyn.

Thus this book speaks with complete conviction.* Other sensational accounts by famous emigrés, such as Avtorkhanov (who offers lugubrious stories about the circumstances of Stalin's death), are carefully weighed against the evidence and rightly dismissed. Stalin's role as a war leader, and his post-war honours, are painstakingly analysed and set in the context of important testimony that has hitherto been unavailable.

Apparently there were two documents still kept locked in Stalin's desk at the time of his death. One was Lenin's final note threatening to end all relations with him because of his hectoring behaviour to Krupskaya. The other was a short letter from Tito, which read quite simply:

"Comrade Stalin: I request that you stop sending terrorists to Yugoslavia to kill me. We have already caught seven men, one with a revolver, another with a grenade, the third with a bomb, etc. If this does not stop, I will send one man to Moscow and there will be no need to send another."

Medvedev on Trotsky is bound to be interesting. He finds the founder of the Red Army to have been mistaken on many counts, and many of his criticisms carry considerable weight. He thinks that Trotsky's attitude to the New Economic Policy was not justifiable, and that, if Trotsky was right about the exhaus-

---

*Ellen de Kadt, the translator, offers an almost impeccable English version, although she must clearly be mistaken in speaking of Stalin's plot for an invasion of Yugoslavia from Armenia, which seems obviously a slip of the pen for Bulgaria. We know of various frighteningly large troop concentrations on the Bulgarian frontier at times marking various low points in Soviet-Yugoslav relations, but not of projected airlifts from Asia.

tion of the Soviet working class during the civil war, this implied a strategy to give respite to the fatigued, rather than making newer and more strenuous demands upon them.

He cites from Soviet witnesses, up to now unreported in the West, remarkable testimony about Trotsky's capacities as a war leader, but he dissents from the view widely current among Trotskyists about his qualifications for peace-time leadership.

At the same time, some of his judgments might be modified in the light of materials that are generally available in the West, but not in the Soviet Union. As Ernest Mandel writes, in his exposition of Trotsky's key ideas,* Medvedev has made "the only honest attempt to write about Trotsky in the contemporary Soviet Union . . . and there is visible progress from book to book". Mandel is right to say that a Soviet scholar "is cut off from many sources", and it is to be hoped that his own short work soon reaches Medvedev in a language he can read. It is a sharp and valuable exposition that makes a serious effort to distinguish between major strategic thinking and conjunctural short-run predictions. Mandel's Trotsky is not a cult figure, and is presented as having been mistaken on a variety of matters.

Yet, although much of it will influence Soviet scholars, when they can read it, I do not think Roy Medvedev will have to revise his judgment about Trotsky's last thoughts on the post-Second World War evolution of the Soviet Union. For that matter, Trotsky's simultaneous forecast about the exhaustion of parliamentary democracy in the capitalist world was wildly wrong, and has remained so for three decades.

If the current world crisis rehabilitates aspects of this view (since it is clear that mass unemployment is not readily compatible with democratic institutions), it will be a mistake to follow much crude Marxian thinking on this issue by assuming that the years from 1945 to 1975 simply never happened, or constitute 'an exception' to more general dismal trends. Another such 'exception' would see us through a lifetime!

On the other hand, a collapse of parliamentary government in the West in the last quarter of the 20th century might also precipitate the end of all human civilisation, since the danger of nuclear war in such circumstances would almost certainly be fiercely augmented. Moreover, there is a great deal of reason to

* *Trotsky* by Ernest Mandel. New Left Books, 1979.

believe that the successive experience of fascism, Stalinism and the development of welfare capitalism have welded working people more firmly than ever to parliamentary institutions, however radically they may wish to modify them to embrace participatory socialist democratic reforms. Détente and the expansion of democracy are vital slogans both East and West, and Medvedev, holed up in his Moscow fastness, has a live and burning appreciation of this truth.

Two other new works have arrived to mark the centenary.

Ronald Segal has written a gripping and well-structured biography of Trotsky,* which is a marked improvement on all the previous one-volume lives to appear in recent years. For all that, it does not adequately take on board much relevant modern writing, notably Cohen's study of Bukharin. Nor does it add much to Isaac Deutscher's still irreplaceable trilogy.

Neither does Robert Wistrich, whose more critical book** has the merit of brevity, and an interesting shift of focus. Wistrich is also the author of a study on *Revolutionary Jews from Marx to Trotsky,* and he uses this vantage point to make some acute observations about his subject, and some that seem more farfetched.

If the 'quasi-religious fervour and fanaticism with which Trotsky inspired the Red Army' was 'reminiscent of Cromwell's Puritan Ironsides', we are bound to ask why, and in what it was reminiscent. Wistrich sees this fervour as a negation of Jewish reflective intellectuality. But an historian steeped in English nonconformity might with equal one-sidedness see in it a negation of bourgeois individualism.

Surely the Ironsides and the Red Army shared their fervour, which was for a new moral world, just as they shared a ruthlessly practical style of leadership that was professional to its fingertips, as a result of the exigencies of civil war. But these were not in either case to prevent a return to earlier doubts and disputations once the military threat was past.

What all these books — for, against and neutral — are beginning to tell us about Trotsky is that, flawed though it may be, his legacy is being valued more greatly with each passing decade.

About Stalin, as Roy Medvedev quite properly says, even if

---

*   *The Tragedy of Leon Trotsky* by Ronald Segal. Hutchinson, 1978.
**   *Trotsky: Fate of a Revolutionary* by Robert Wistrich. Robson, 1979.

"there no longer appears any threat of rehabilitation", the continued struggle "against Stalin and neo-Stalinism in all its manifestations, whether open or veiled, continues to be one of the most important problems facing the world communist movement".

II

"He tried, on his own terms, to be equal to his time. Even those who cannot heed his word may recognise that Leon Trotsky, in his power and his fall, is one of the Titans of our century."

This is Irving Howe's judgment, in a clearly written little book* which is surely one of the best of the most useful series in which it appears. Baruch Knei-Paz would scarcely disagree, although his book,** also entirely readable, is anything but little, numbering over 600 pages. Neither of these careful authors is in any way an uncritical fan of his subject, and both books have been written in an attempt to compass Trotsky's rich legacy of ideas in a sceptical and discriminating way. I hope both will be read with equal attention, because some of the themes addressed by Trotsky, even where we find him to have been most in the wrong, remain dominant in the contemporary world, and no relevant socialism will emerge with real force until the unfinished intellectual tasks undertaken by Trotsky are taken forward into our own time.

Both these books will assist in this process precisely inasmuch as they are critical, and both are evidence of an important prospect that the dialogue about the strengths and limitations of Trotsky's politics may soon begin to involve people far outside the limited circles within which this discussion has run until comparatively recently. Howe, in keeping with the purpose of the library to which he contributes, offers an introductory text, judiciously combining elements of biography and debate.

He also takes issue with Trotsky's biographer, Isaac Deutscher, in a section which I find distinctly unfair. The argument turns upon some thoughts expressed in a sad essay, written in 1939, when Trotsky was contemplating the possibility that his perspective of a liberatory political revolution in the USSR

---

*   Irving Howe: *Trotsky*. Fontana Modern Masters, 1978.
**   Baruch Knei-Paz: *The Social and Political Thoughts of Leon Trotsky. Oxford University Press, 1978.*

alongside the anti-capitalist revolutions of the West might be falsified: if it should fail, he wrote

"it is self-evident that a new minimum programme would be required — to defend the interests of the slaves of the totalitarian bureaucratic system."

Howe then quotes Deutscher's commentary upon this:

"Having lived all his life with the conviction that . . . history was on the side of those who struggled for the emancipation of the exploited and oppressed, he now entreated his disciples to remain on the side of the exploited . . . even if history and all scientific certainties were against them. He, at any rate, would be with Spartacus, not with Pompey and the Caesars."

Surprisingly, Howe then concludes that this passage indicates that Deutscher disapproved of this moral commitment. Deutscher, he thinks "never learned that unpredictable as human history may be, history is a bitch".

To the contrary, it seems absolutely plain that whatever villainies men fall into, over and again time reveals virtue for what it really was, so that in this sense only, human history is completely predictable. New rogues will probably emerge continually, but truly honourable and decent behaviour cannot ever be wiped out of human memories, which is all that history, in the last analysis, ever is. In this sense, Irving Howe himself, in rightly lauding Trotsky as the pioneer opponent and analyst of Stalinism, provides in his own judgments clear testimony that history is not at all a bitch. We may be absolutely confident that Isaac Deutscher, whatever gestures he made to the 'scientific certainties', entirely endorsed Trotsky's commitment to the *moral* certainty which invariably aligned his subject with Spartacus, however long the odds against him.

In truth, what people take for the moral certainties are usually arguable, and sometimes plainly wrong: but they are nothing like as vulnerable to fashion and vacillation as the alleged verities of 'science', above all, those of political science. What makes scholars write books about Trotsky is not that this and that detail of his social philosophy is beyond or not beyond reproach, but that his life was an integral one, of a piece with the needs of his time, just as Irving Howe has concluded.

Of far greater importance than Howe's introductory book, though, is the ponderous study by Knei-Paz. This suffers from over-explicitness, in that every little detail of the argument has to be explained, and sometimes at a level which can hardly be necessary, since any potential readers of this book will need, before they even start, a fair degree of familiarity with the period and persons involved in the Trotsky story. Even so, Knei-Paz has given us invaluable material which is available nowhere else in the English language, especially in the documentation of the crucial and bitter arguments which went on between Trotsky and Lenin, in the years between their first encounter in London, and the tumult of 1917. Few who read this account with the care it deserves will accept Trotsky's subsequent judgment that he had been simply wrong in all the salient details of the controversy on Party organisation. In particular, Knei-Paz offers an extensive summary of the tract *Our Political Tasks*. A volume containing this and related writings is an overdue requirement for scholars and others concerned with this fascinating issue.

In an inadvertent commentary on Howe's criticism of Deutscher, Knei-Paz points up, towards the end of this remarkable study, the conscious parallel made by Trotsky between Marxism and Calvinism, in his book *Whither England?*

"We may with perfect right", he had written, "draw an analogy between the doctrine of predestination in the Puritan Revolution and the role of Marxism in the proletarian revolution. In both cases, the great efforts put forth are not based on subjective caprice, but on a cast-iron causal law, mystically distorted in the one case, scientifically founded in the other."

'Caprice' has in fact got more to offer than Trotsky was then willing to admit, and how much more may partly be discerned in the exchange reported above, in discussing Howe's brief argument. I am powerfully reminded of another view, set down, at the very time of Trotsky's own sufferings, by another victim, Antonio Gramsci, then locked away in one of Mussolini's prisons:

> "With regard to the historical role played by the fatalist interpretation of Marxism, one could pronounce a funeral eulogy of it, vindicating its usefulness for a certain period, but precisely because of this urging the necessity of burying it with all honours. Its role could be likened to that of the theory of grace and predestination for the beginnings of the modern world, which, however, culminated in classical German philosophy with its conception of freedom as the awareness of necessity. It has been a popular substitute for the cry 'God wills it . . .'"

Gramsci was right. However, under the cry 'God wills it', we may recollect, not only many wrongs done, but some few generous and brave lives lived.

III

Yet another life of Trotsky. This one,* not quite the worst yet, is nonetheless not recommended. It is difficult to see why it was written, since it offers very little information which was not already available when it was prepared. Indeed, it does not explore some of the most important materials on recent Russian history which have appeared since the completion of the monumental Deutscher biography, so that there is little awareness of modern samizdat writings, no detailed consideration of the various testimonies from Roy Medvedev and his co-thinkers, no reference to the recent work of Western scholars like Professor Day, and in short, no reason outside that of alternative political preferences to choose this book rather than that.

It is possible that Deutscher's book, already available a score of years, could be somewhat updated, or could be opposed by an equally serious alternative estimate of its subject. But there is little reason to spend time reading Mr Payne when Deutscher is at hand, and none for substituting this new book for Deutscher's old one. In biographical matters, Deutscher's three volumes cover almost everything more fully, and, yes, more dispassionately, than does Payne's single one. When we move outside the details of Trotsky's life, and peep into the contents of his mind, there is no possible comparison whatever.

Slipshod is not an adequate word with which to characterise Robert Payne's attempts to summarise Trotsky's ideas. Considering *Literature and Revolution,* he writes: "What he wanted was 'socialist realism' although this combination of words had not come into existence." How anyone could even leaf through this book and come up with such a conclusion is difficult to imagine: but to make matters worse, Mr Payne later quotes from the surrealist manifesto which Trotsky was to draft with André Breton, which characterised official Soviet art as "bad choruses of well-disciplined liars", and insisted that "every free creation is styled 'fascist' by the Stalinists". The incongruity of these sentiments with socialist realism is not even noted by the author, who seems not to mind that his book contradicts itself, never mind the facts. In the same argument, Payne speaks of Trotsky, "for the first and last time in his life" bestowing his approval on Christianity, when he considered how "The Christian myth

---

* Robert Payne, *The Life and Death of Trotsky.* W.H. Allen, 1978.

unified the monumental art of the middle ages''. Perhaps we may doubt whether many bishops would regard such an appreciation as 'approval': but if it is indeed approving, there are then many similar instances of approbation in Trotsky's writings from his *Autobiography* through to his last papers. He had, for instance, a good word for the protestant revolutionaries in Cromwell's England, including their regrettable doctrine of predestination; and he spoke warmly of jesuits when he was discussing morality with Professor Dewey. It is no secret at all that the Bolsheviks were atheists: but Trotsky was by no means uninterested in religious thought, particularly in that of oppressed groupings.

When he quotes, Mr Payne frequently leaves out the remarks which give meaning to what is being cited. Thus, in reproducing a remarkable assault on Ramsay MacDonald, he does not explain that MacDonald was under reproach for preaching 'evolution' rather than revolution. In the pursuit of this dispute, Trotsky's vignette has a point which Mr Payne (who omits all contextual explanation) has plainly failed to grasp:

"British pigeon fanciers, by means of artificial selection, achieve special varieties with a continually shortening beak. But there comes a moment when the beak of a new stock is so short that the poor creature is unequal to breaking the egg shell and the young pigeon perishes, a sacrifice to compulsory restraint from revolutionary activities, and a stop is put to the further progress of varieties of short bills. If our memory is not at fault, MacDonald can read about this in Darwin. Having entered upon MacDonald's favourite course of analogies with the organic world, one can say that the political art of the British bourgeois consists of shortening the revolutionary beak of the proletariat, and so not allowing him to pierce the shell of the capitalist State."

"The metaphor is too complex", says Mr Payne, ". . . he handles it badly; the argument becomes grotesque''. On the contrary; the metaphor is devastating, it is brilliantly controlled, and to show wherein it implies erroneous conclusions is to undertake a labour of political analysis which is far beyond the capacities of Mr Payne, just as it surpassed the limits of Ramsay MacDonald's powers. Poor MacDonald was to live out the rest of his life as if he were possessed by the urge to prove Trotsky right in spite of all contrary evidence. It was not for nothing that Bernard Shaw spoke with near reverence of Trotsky's satirical powers.

What the various Trotsky archivists should do for us now is, first to discourage 'popular' books like this one, which add little or nothing but confusion to the issues; second, to encourage detailed treatment of particular episodes and arguments, starting with the period from 1905 to 1917; and third, to make available some of the still untranslated material which has not been accessible (outside a handful of libraries) for far too long. Only after this has been done do I seriously expect to read a life of Trotsky which will have a chance to improve upon that by Isaac Deutscher.

IV

"Of Christ's 12 apostles, Judas alone proved to be a traitor. But if he had acquired power he would have represented the other 11 apostles as traitors, and also all the lesser apostles, whom Luke numbers as 70."

Trotsky recorded this thought in the unfinished manuscript of his biography of Stalin, shortly before he was murdered. Unfinished though it was, this fascinating work has certainly retained its relevance, and some of the new biographers who have stepped forward to explain the Great Butcher's story are candid and perceptive enough to register that fact.

Yet here we have three brand new "lives" of the Soviet dictator, all massive and meticulously studied, each of which, in its own way, is an attempt to refute the basic assumption of Trotsky that his opponent was "a creation of the machine", a perfect spokesman for the dull bureaucracy which emerged within the Soviet Union during the stalemate of the revolution in Western Europe.

Ronald Hingley,* whose book is in many ways the best general introduction of the three, sums up this view in an apt quotation from E.H. Carr: "More than almost any other great man in history, Stalin illustrates the thesis that circumstances make the man, not the man the circumstances." Hingley strenuously contests this judgment, and both Adam B. Ulam**and Robert C. Tucker [†] would seem to share his view. At least, they put a higher value on the capacity of their subject for political manoeuvre and manipulation than could any of his defeated opponents.

---

*   *Joseph Stalin: Man and Legend.* Ronald Hingley. Hutchinson, 1974.
** *Stalin: the Man and his Era.* Adam B. Ulman. Allen Lane, 1974.
†   *Stalin as Revolutionary.* Robert C. Tucker. Chatto and Windus, 1974.

This raises a very complex question, which easily provokes simples answers. To those whom Trotsky derided as "worshippers of the accomplished fact", Stalin's "greatness" is established by the fact that he displayed the apparent capacity to humiliate an opposition which was cleverer, nicer or wickeder (according to the particular standpoint of the commentator) than he himself. So, like a good cannibal, he is assumed to have absorbed into his own person the virtues (or vices, if one takes a misanthropic view) of those over whom he had triumphed.

To those whose values preclude reverence for power as an end in itself, to the insurgent temperaments and to those who adjudge progress in terms of the widest liberation of personal capacities for development, things appear very differently.

Perhaps the most interesting new life of Stalin would be one which thoroughly understood the horrors he unleashed, and yet consistently endeavoured to take Carr as a guide and present the villain as the victim of the social pressures to which he had been exposed. In a certain sense, Robert Tucker has been trying to write this book, but he has failed because his understanding of social pressures is refracted through a narrowly psychological prism.

The most "Stalinist" of these portraits is the one by Adam Ulam, who still vibrates to the tunes of the cold war. Even though Ulam ranges himself on what he sees as the opposite side to that of his sitter, this inevitably means that he shares some of Stalin's basic preconceptions. This portrait thus presents an aggressive tyrant in the world of international relations, but, sharp though it is, tends to give the monster a charitable verdict when it concerns his domestic affairs.

Accordingly, Ulam offers us a long polemic with Roy Medvedev about the assassination of Kirov, which event precipitated the purge trials and mass deportations and executions of Party members. Medvedev's own account is detailed and careful, and he tentatively concludes that Stalin's role in the murder was fishy, to say the least of it.

Ulam gives Stalin the benefit of an unnecessarily large quota of doubt on this matter. He discusses part of Medvedev's valuable evidence, but by no means all of it, and then goes on to speculate that since Yagoda, the secret police chief at the time, was soft on Bukharin, he was therefore not to be trusted with such a delicate killing.

But there is a fair amount of evidence that Yagoda's fear of his master weighed considerably heavier with him than his fondness for anyone else, and Medvedev certainly reveals sufficient detail about the eccentricities of first the OGPU and then its successor the NKVD, before and after the assassination, to make the presumption of Stalin's involvement at least as credible as the suspicion that President Nixon knew more about Watergate than he was willing to admit.

Naturally, both of the authors whose works cover the period offer a great deal of data about the subsequent terror. Yet it is impossible to believe that the last word has yet been written on this question, because the freeze which has descended on contemporary Soviet literature and historiography means, quite simply, that the main flow of evidence is yet to come. What we have seen of the current attempts to examine the question, in *samizdat,* indicates something of the dreadful indictment which will one day be tabled.

Meantime, these biographers also raise far less important, but still interesting, questions. Ulam speaks of Stalin employing "ghost" writers. Did he write his own books?

Roy Medvedev has recently intimated than an important part of *The Foundations of Leninism* may have been ghosted by F.A. Ksenofontov, and the recent memoirs of an anonymous "Bolshevik-Leninist" (published in *samizdat* by Monad Press, New York) claim that Stalin tried to persuade Aleksandr Slepkov, a brilliant young follower of Bukharin, to undertake a similar role, alternating stiff doses of penal exile and ingratiating personal interviews in the attempt to "persuade" him. Slepkov was not suborned and paid for his integrity with his life.

But what of Ksenofontov? The "Bolshevik-Leninist" is quite certain that he was Stalin's pen, going so far as to assert that he wrote "whole volumes" of Stalin's *Collected Works.* Tucker disputes this, and offers some evidence that *Foundations of Leninism* differs substantially from an admittedly similar book published at about the same time by Ksenofontov. It is an intriguing question, if only because it is possible that the true believers have, all the time, been preaching Marxism-Leninism-Ksenofontovism.

The real Stalin was undoubtedly an evil customer, and undoubtedly each of these heavy books has some real light to throw on parts of his record. But there will be many more books before someone gets it right enough for us to close the Stalin file. Meanwhile, his ghost still walks, as if to mock Karl Marx's spectre, still creatively haunting away.

The only thing we can say, with complete confidence, is that struggle between these spirits will remain intransigent to the last degree, and that the one can prevail only at the expense of the other.

Chapter 9

Communism in Britain:
Tales of Innocence and Experience

I
The Experience of Harry Pollitt

Harry Pollitt led the British Communist Party from August 1929 until May 1956. For all but three years of that time, the Party faithfully belched on every occasion Stalin found wind in his tummy, and Harry himself dutifully did his hiccups through every turn but one. The three years from 1953 onwards did not reveal the Communists in a new state of grace, but they saw Stalin himself translated to a warmer clime.

During the Pollitt years, Soviet policy went in a series of drastic phases, some of which, viewed from a Leftist perspective in England, were quite rational, even laudable, while others were palpably not so. It was, therefore, no little feat to build up a staunch cadre of activists (which multiplied itself tenfold during the period in question) dedicated to supporting the Soviet power through thin and thick.

British communism owed a great deal to its spokesman. He could almost unfailingly translate turgid directives from paralytic cominternese into a crisp, and sometimes resonant, Lancashire idiom. He worked hard and, even allowing for ghosting, was a fertile pamphleteer. As an orator, no one could possibly ghost for him: he maintained his capacity to fill halls tightly full, even through the most dismal years of the cold war. He fought his share of good fights, and these helped to carry the Party through its bad ones.

John Mahon, the author of this biography,* was a pious man, about whom the worst thing his enemies could say was that he lived on carrots and pure devotion, and washed himself clean in the dew every morning. Now they will be able to say that he also wrote this book. Of course, it was reasonable for the Party to

---

* *Harry Pollitt* by John Mahon. Lawrence & Wishart, 1976.

pay its debts. Six hundred heavy pages, including five separate indices and a list of almost all the newspaper articles ever signed by the late leader is one way of doing this. But it is certainly not the *best* way for a party which is genuinely trying to re-evaluate its history and rediscover a commitment to socialist humanism.

This book will persuade few among the unconverted, for whom the undoubted fact that Harry Pollitt loved his mother will not outweigh his shortcomings on a larger stage than that of family life. Neither will it enlighten the true believers, since it will provide them with no mechanism of argument by which to enlarge their diminishing circles. For all the laboured painstaking which is invested in it, the work comes off the press as a heavy anti-climax.

What was it that took this likeable and clever boilermaker and turned him into an important political figure? What objectives did he set himself, and how far did he feel he had realised them, at the end of a life full of sacrifice, hurtful compromise and intense effort? How was it that a young libertarian, weaned on Shelley, William Morris, Kropotkin and Paul Lafargue, could become a tight-lipped apologist for crass tyranny? John Mahon doesn't ask that sort of question.

Pollitt's tragedy was part of that cosmic disaster which swallowed up the hopeful prospects of the International Labour Movement: the rise of Stalinism. His story cries out for sympathetic historical treatment, precisely inasmuch as Pollitt seems to have been himself a decent, often kindly, man. Yet he succeeded to the post of general secretary of the CPGB just as Stalin had crushed his Left opposition, and was about to tear apart his critics on the 'Right'.

His ascendancy was linked, indeed indissolubly cemented, to that of Rajani Palme Dutt, who seems to have been the very prototype of frigid casuistry and unfeeling moral opportunism. Possibly Dutt at home was kind to cats, but in his public persona he displayed only a remorseless affection for power and a total lack of humane conscience. He praised first Lenin, then Trotsky, then Bukharin, then Stalin, then Khrushchev; each with a calculated and impartial disregard for any embarrassing discontinuities in their behaviour.

Jokingly, Mahon tells us, Pollitt once confessed that he and Dutt embodied a marriage of theory and practice, Pollitt himself providing the theory. Certainly, this extraordinary alliance is well worth literary exploration. It seems that, like many another victim of matrimony, Harry Pollitt hated this political spouse with the unflagging animus which is born of, and perpetually renewed by, dependence. About such matters, Mahon is discretion itself. To an outsider, it sometimes looks like Jekyll and Hyde in reverse, as if the villainous Mr Dutt had steamed away in his laboratory of applied dogmatics in order to invent Dr Nice-Guy Pollitt: yet, of course, it cannot really be as simple as that.

But to John Mahon, it was simply a fraternity of two just men. Any truth we find about this fascinating relationship is firmly wedged between the lines of this ponderous account. Briefly, at the beginning of the Second World War, the partnership was sundered, when Pollitt held to the opinion that it was an anti-fascist struggle, while Dutt quickly asserted the official comintern view that it was simply another conflict of rival imperialisms. The bare events are here recorded, but precious little else. Mahon is not an historian to wash dirty linen at all, leave alone publicly. He is not even keen to display clean linen, if he thinks it likely to remind people of the existence of dirt.

Yet the events in question took place half a normal life-span ago, and even the secrets of the Cabinet papers have begun to emerge since then. Surely *someone,* if only a relative or neighbour, said *something* just a trifle indiscreet and open about it all, or might recall an unofficial thought?

Nobody in this book lets untoward ideas into their heads about the Soviet Union, either. All Stalin's crimes are unreported, indeed, unremarked, by John Mahon, until his narrative reaches the 20th Congress of the CPSU, in 1956. Then we arrive at Stalin's "serious theoretical and political errors". Pollitt, we are told, "without any attempts to minimise or excuse, recognised that the exposure of Stalin's mistakes . . . had come as an unexpected shock to the whole CPGB". This, to put it politely, is whitewash.

In the letters of Pat Dooley, a communist organiser who returned from Prague to Rumania to England in 1953, we read: "I told Pollitt, Campbell and Gollan all that is now being said . . . Pollitt didn't want to know — he treated me as a naïve boy who has just heard the facts of life — and smiled at me — told me to keep quiet, don't talk 'while at home' and go back and don't get mixed up in anything!"

While John Mahon includes various minute comments on unimportant 'falsifications' in his dossier, he remains silent about Dooley's revelations. He does record Pollitt's early affection for Rose Cohen, but we have to go to a footnote to discover that, after her migration to the Soviet Union, "some years later her husband and she was arrested *(sic)*. This was a great sorrow to Harry, who did not believe her guilty, and made every effort to get her case reviewed, without result."

Rose Cohen never came out of prison alive. She fell into the 'meatgrinder'. Surely a biography which tells us in detail about its subject's rather boring wanderings in India or Australasia might be expected to tell us exactly what happened to Rose Cohen, and exactly what was done to help her? Some of us would also like to know what the British Communist executive did when it was reported that all the general secretary's best efforts had been ignored. Did they protest? Or was it deemed wiser to 'keep quiet'?

No, this book won't do. Harry Pollitt's life was a riddle, because he was caught up in processes which turned his best efforts into sick parodies of his honest intentions. That riddle could be unravelled, to the benefit of the Labour movement: but only by an intellect more curious and more fastidious than that of John Mahon.

II

The Innocence of Tariq Ali

The dust jacket of Tariq Ali's new book* features pictures of a variety of revolutionary comrades toting loudhailers and microphones, and apparently all talking at once. To judge by the shapes of their faces, they are all saying different things. Perhaps that's why Tariq's photo looks so cross.

In fact, this author is not at all like the rather virulent chap portrayed either on the front of this book, or inside it. He has recently been spending a lot of time campaigning up and down the country against the execution of ex-prime minister Bhutto, even though it is perfectly plain that Bhutto and he have, through all their time up to now, shared remarkably few political opinions. I find all this to Tariq Ali's credit, and feel that for this and many other similar reasons it would be perfectly

* *Tariq Ali: 1968 and After — Inside the Revolution*. Blond and Briggs, 1978.

Tariq Al

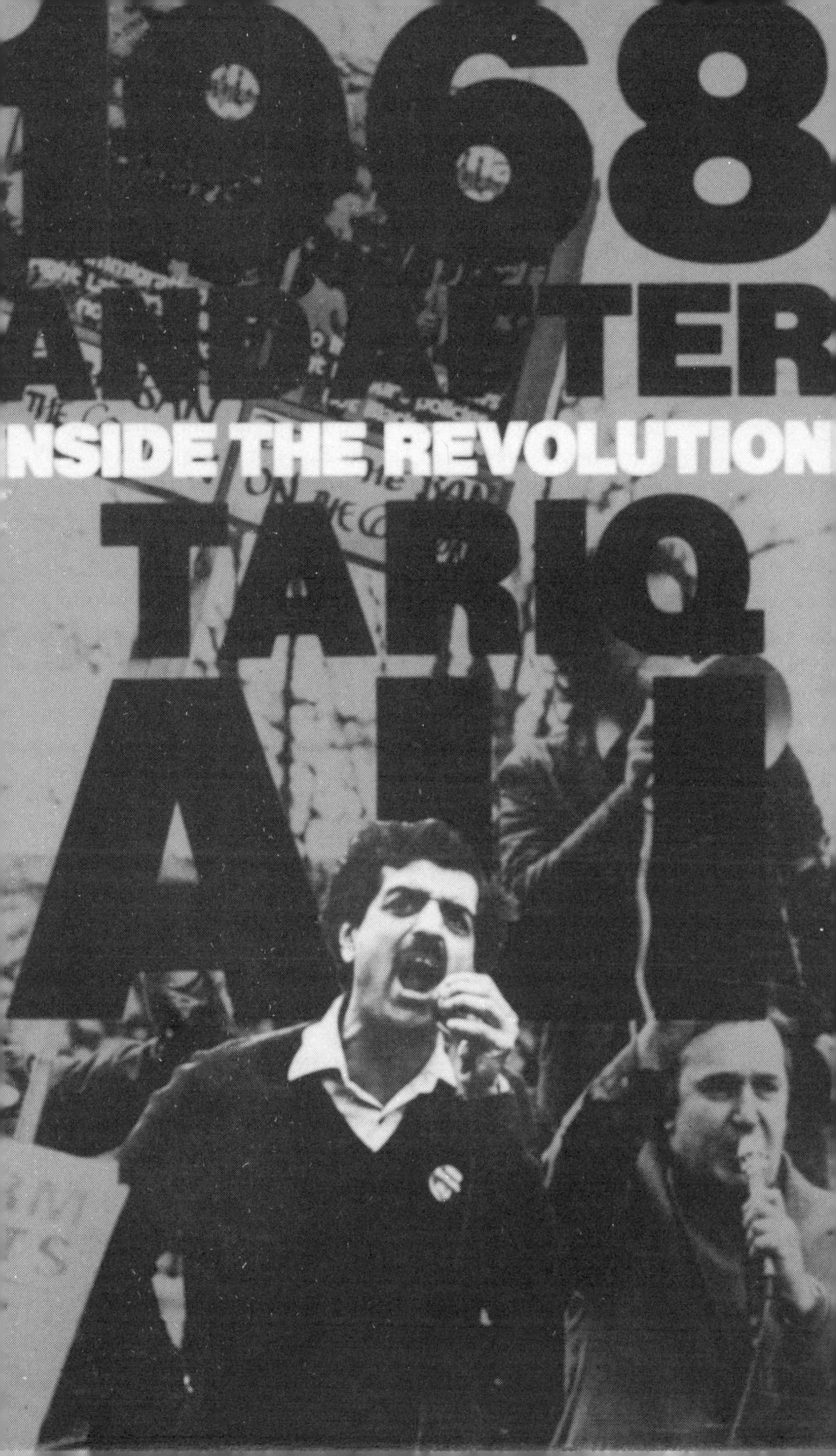
1968
NSIDE THE REVOLUTION
TARIQ
ALI

possible to present him in a far more sympathetic light than that in which he here presents himself.

The trouble is that although he has given his latest work the sub-title 'Inside the Revolution', most of it is about revolutionary events that he was definitely *outside,* not only physically, but to a greater extent than he sees, morally. Apart from a chapter on Britain and some general thoughts on socialism and democracy, this book consists of chapters on Vietnam, France, Czechoslovakia, Chile and Portugal respectively. One lesson he draws from the revolutionary outcome in Vietnam is that the Communists of Italy and France had been wrong after 1945 to shrink before the fear of United States intervention, in holding back from a postwar assault 'for working class power'.

All this is to misconceive, rather more than a little, what a considerable proportion of the wartime communist supporters in these countries intended their parties to do. The resistance against fascism and nazism had not been promoted as a form of soviet-style revolution, but an alliance of forces struggling for the restoration of democratic rights and national independence: and those Trotskyists who counterposed to these goals the hope for a new revolution on the 1917 model, were wrong. They had come to accept a theory which maintained that Capital was so enamoured of the strong State that it was impossible to restore parliamentary democracy for any length of time, that in Europe the American occupying soldiers would soon be generally seen in a similar light to the defeated German armies before them, and that an immediate post-war slump would clinch these reactions. By contrast, since these assumptions were all untrue, the truly 'revolutionary' thing to do in 1945 was to organise for the most audacious and systematic democratic advance throughout industry and society, and to build up a unified socialist agitation to this end. Following the faith however, Trotskyists took themselves to an hermitage for almost two decades, during which time they blamed each other because it was lonely, found wide measures of disagreement about how many revolutionary angels were able to marshall themselves on the pin-point of an objectively favourable situation, fell out fiercely and fought each other to near extinction.

Tariq is, not unnaturally, incurious about such prehistoric affairs, because the revolution *he* is in began to move in 1968 on impulses from Vietnam. After all, his own experience in the

Vietnam Solidarity Campaign was for him a major turning point. But remarkable as was the Vietnamese resistance to French and then American intervention, it had no direct exemplary relevance to any thinkable politics in Europe. Guerrilla war in Vietnam based itself on a secure supporting hinterland which afforded safe refuge and sustenance, and on the convenient benevolent neutrality of an adjacent neighbour. Once people in any part of post-war Europe came to the exchange of angry shots, however, all others in the world would quickly be engulfed in blood and neutrons. The formation of NATO was quite specifically justified in these terms, and this triggered the Warsaw Pact. It soon became apparent that each alliance was primarily concerned with police work in its own territories. Had those frontiers at any point come under effective military or insurrectionary challenge, we would then have been embarking upon the third world war. A considerable trend in Trotskyism faced this fact in the late 'forties, and developed a theory of the inevitability of some such event. Gerry Healy, indeed, published a ghosted tract under the appealing title *The Coming World Showdown*. Recruits for this were difficult to find. This fact vindicates at least one of Tariq Ali's fondest beliefs, which is, as he tells us more than once, faith in the working class.

In the event, Trotskyists of most tendencies were just like everyone else when this fevered prognosis was at last put to the test in the Cuba crisis, and it looked as if the *Coming World Showdown* was about to turn into the *Going World Showdown*. Those who weren't too proud to pray thanked God for Khrushchev, as indeed I do even now whenever I put up a skylark or am otherwise reminded that it is still good to be alive.

Tariq Ali's revolution is happily innocent of many of these problems. It reveals itself in the flush of the May Events in Paris, or in Lisbon during the Portuguese upheaval, and very beautiful they both were. Almost no-one was hurt, a powerful warmth and solidarity were generated, and the long-term effect in each case was not at all negligible. And yet the heart-warming slogan 'Imagination au pouvoir' really means 'no-one in power', and everyone and no-one will vote for that when they see what it practically implies. The struggle for socialism shot forward decades in a few moments when that turbulent spirit revealed itself again, because choking routine became a poor choice rather than an inevitable lifestyle, once people were able to let their minds breathe. Yet the agencies of the change which then became thinkable are still being sought, tentatively, experimentally, in battles and compromises of a hundred kinds, wherever in France or Portugal (or anywhere else) democracy sees a chance to grow, or needs to hold a corner temporarily gained.

This book scarcely deals with the politics of this process, because it still tends to see the revolution as a day of reckoning rather than the long tug-o'-war which the nuclear stalemate determines it must be. Of course, our side cannot gain an inch without courage and dedication: but neither can it begin to develop these necessary qualities if it does not reach for the political categories within which it may begin to contend with the real conditions of modern politics. Such categories could do worse than start with May in Paris and Spring in Prague, but they must also then be worked through all our shared accumulation of democratic experience.

Tariq Ali has learned from difficult experience that only a democratic revolution could approach the socialism he wants to create, and so his new book is more thoughtful than was his earlier essay on *The Coming British Revolution*. But the move from such worthy principles to practical proposals is complex and difficult, or perhaps it might well have been made already. As a searcher in the labyrinth, I did not find anything very helpful in this book's map, which fuzzes at precisely the points where only clarity will do.

Is socialism, as a short option, then, impossible? Not at all: but it is more than ever contingent on international actions, international commitments. When Tariq Ali applies his undoubted zeal for this approach to the existing real working class movements which are currently constrained within the present real balance of military power, he really will move inside the revolution. Now, with the compass he has to hand, he has unfortunately produced a book which will soon be out of date, if not quite as quickly as was his last.

However, we need not fear that he will be inhibited about producing his next.

Chapter 10

Eurocommunism in the West

Some wit has already told us that "a spectre is haunting communism: the spectre of Europe". The distinctive evolution of the French, Italian, Spanish, Swedish, Belgian and British communist parties since the Soviet and allied invasion of Czechoslovakia has certainly resulted in distancing them from 'the Russian model', and has to some extent brought them together as a block with a degree of common policy. This should not be exaggerated: none of the parties of the nine present EEC countries is in complete agreement with any of the others on its attitudes to the institutions of the Commission; the French and Spanish parties are at loggerheads about the inclusion of Spain within the Market's framework; the Italian 'historic compromise' contrasts markedly with development of the 'common programme' of the French Left. Notwithstanding such dissensions, the policies of these parties taken together are indeed markedly different from, say, those of the Bulgarians, or the West Germans, or the Danes. If eurocommunism is a weak term, it is not because there is nothing distinct about the attitudes of the most important European parties, but because they share such attitudes not only within our familiar latitudes, but also with Australians, or even with the Japanese.

What characteristics mark this family of parties apart? First, their evolution beyond what Togliatti called "polycentrism" to a real degree of critical detachment from the influence of the Soviet Union. All the eurocommunists criticise the current repressions in the USSR, regret the freezing of de-Stalinisation, and are at pains to assert their commitment to an autonomous, distinct 'road to socialism'. Socialism in the colours of France, or Japan, is presented as a process of its own, in its own right.

Secondly, each of these parties has overtly or tacitly, renounced such concepts as 'the dictatorship of the proletariat'. Constitutional change, linking parliamentary and non-parliamentary forms of democratic action, has become a general doctrine.

Each of the interesting books we are considering approaches these two central questions in a different way. Santiago Carrillo*, as a major figure in eurocommunism (and a favourite target of the Soviet leadership) is concerned to establish both the novelty and the continuity of his doctrine. He makes much of the formative experiences of the popular front, and is able to cite an important letter from Stalin, Molotov and Voroshilov, which shows that, way back in 1936, all these figures were well-prepared to espouse highly heterodox assumptions about the progress of the Spanish revolution.

Yet, of course, if one takes the doctrines of Stalin very seriously, one can find abundant evidence in his writing for many contradictory views, including the proposition that there is little new in the politics of Berlinguer and Marchais, let alone those of their British supporters. After all, in his brief speech at the 19th Congress of the CPSU, Stalin *did* say:

> "the banner of bourgeois-democratic liberties has been thrown overboard. I believe it is you, the representatives of the communist and democratic parties, who will have to raise this banner and carry it forward, if you want to gather around you the majority of the people. There is nobody else to raise it."

The cynicism of such words, from the architect of *Gulag,* does not in the least detract from the fact that their author was very happy to encourage the British communists to experiment with the prototype of their present programme, 'eurocommunist' though it may now be considered. Critics of the Italian communists are not shy to point out that some of their contemporary catchwords could be found on the hoardings of their Hungarian co-thinkers during the last free elections to be held before Rakosi's salami tactics sliced up every vestige of 'bourgeois-democratic liberties' in the fateful days leading up to the insurrection of 1956. From his side Ernest Mandel** identifies the second commitment of eurocommunism (to peaceful change) as a straightforward inheritance from Stalin, and sees the first (to autonomy from the USSR) as a reflection of libertarian working class pressures which would severely penalise any authoritarian

* *Eurocommunism and the State,* Santiago Carrillo. Lawrence and Wishart, 1977.
** *From Stalinism to Eurocommunism.* Ernest Mandel. NLB, 1978.

regression by communists in any of the democratic countries.

In this one sense, Mandel is right. You cannot, as old Heraclitus told us, step into the same river twice. Whatever may be the wishes of political leaders, a vast workers' movement from Bari up to Aberdeen is not in the least willing to endorse, or even tolerate, the 'throwing overboard' of the 'banner of bourgeois-democratic liberties'. If such liberties are ever found to be inadequate or unreal, they will only be replaceable by real and greater ones.

The challenge of eurocommunism is not to be found in its current programmatic statements, which will prove transitory. It is to be found in the growing independence of important mass organisations from a hitherto crippling body of dogmas, which positive fact can only open out new perspectives of change.

Santiago Carrillo traces out the parameters of such euro-communism with a telling quotation from Henry Kissinger:

> "There are people who think that we are too intransigent in our attitude towards these Western communist parties. But we cannot encourage the progress of these parties nor permit the setting of a precedent in which, by our inaction, we have facilitated the success of a communist party. *The extent to which such a party follows Moscow's line is unimportant. Even if Portugal had followed the Italian model, we would still have been opposed.* It is not just because Cunhal is a Stalinist that we are in opposition. Even the impact of an Italian Communist Party that seemed to be governing effectively would be devastating — on France and on NATO too.
>
> It is difficult to see how we could have NATO discussions if these various communist parties of Western Europe did achieve control of governments. We could, as with China, perhaps have parallel policies. But the alliance, as it is now, could not survive. *The Western alliance always had an importance beyond military security.*"

Carrillo rightly stresses that the United States is not over-interested in the extent to which communists follow, or fail to follow, Moscow: the Kissinger doctrine, for instance, would undoubtedly wish the Yugoslavs to be more tractable in their relations with the Soviet Union, since this would help to stabilise the wider region, whose potential for turbulence is a nuisance to both major powers. What the Americans do *not* want, Carrillo insists, is any real change in the West European social system.

It seems rather plain that the Americans (under Carter no less than Kissinger) were fiercely determined to maintain all possible pressures against the entry of Italian Communists even to a coalition share in their government. Nonetheless, paradoxically, such a development would be very scarcely more welcome in Moscow than Washington. If the Prague Spring might have upset every authority in the East, how much more would the triumph of even the most restricted Italian communist governmental participation? Conversely, democratic communism in Czechoslovakia would have had instant repercussions in the West, at least in France and Italy. The fact is that those who dominate each of the great blocs which sunder Europe have a marked interest in stability before almost all other considerations, and that all the smaller constituent nationalities of such blocs are expected, by their respective protectors, to know their permissible bounds even without being told of them.

The shrewdest politicians in Europe inhabit the frontier areas, where these realities are dreadfully alive. Chancellor Kreisky lives in a country in which each of the four post-war powers has a right by treaty to intervene if order is imperilled. President Tito presides over a nation of little nations, with great diversities between more and less developed areas, and constant difficulties from outside-sponsored irridentists and even terrorists. The Italian communists know that any rupture in the Yugoslav polity would fearfully affect their own political structure.

Stacked behind the diplomatic spokesmen, these political leaders can plainly see the shadows of great nuclear arsenals, steadily augmenting. If ever there was a need for the rebirth of the movement for nuclear disarmament, on a truly European scale, it would be now that all the signs emerge of a new frenzied twist to the arms race, forced into ever deadlier fields by the insecurities of the Western slump and the recurrence of mass unemployment in the most developed capitalist economies. Such a movement cannot possibly develop under the hegemony of either power, since it would challenge the felt interests of both. Neither is arming with the intention of a pre-emptive strike against the other, since each comprehends the finality of such a move. But both are pressed by their own insecurities, by the fears engendered within, on the one side, a repressive political system which faces the prospect of atrophy, punctuated by recurrent political crises, and on the other side, an economic turmoil which has already begun disastrously and shows no signs of abatement.

All this is news of peril for all humanity. We should do well to listen to Tito's warnings, given to the recent 11th Congress of the Yugoslav communists.

> "The problem of disarmament is one of the overriding issues today, and it is closely bound up with overall developments in foreign affairs, particularly as regards international peace and security. Thanks above all to the activities of the non-aligned countries, there is a growing conviction in the world that international peace and security cannot be maintained permanently on the strength of a balance of forces, military might or bloc divisions.
> "The arms race is assuming global proportions, and it is safe to say that there are few countries which have not been affected by it in one way or another. However, this arms race — which is becoming increasingly dangerous because of the introduction of new and even more lethal weapons systems — is dominated by the rivalry of the military powers, notably the nuclear powers, and military blocs in general."

Facing this threat, we have, if we will use it, one hopeful resource, which is the potential of the vast working class movements of Western Europe, fragmented as they are. The workers' parties and trade unions of this sub-continent have not been fundamentally defeated since the end of the Second World War, and even in those countries which were peripherally submerged under fascist and other varieties of strong States, they have made a remarkable recovery. Together, they could become a prodigious force. Separate, they will find themselves more and more inadequate to meet the multi-national strains under which they will be brought. The over-riding problem of European socialist strategy is that of how to secure a real convergence between the democratic trends within the socialist and communist movements, asserting the autonomy of the interests of the working population of the whole area. Already it is obvious that the old divisions have become an impediment to practical defensive actions, to say nothing about their obstruction of the overall advancement of democratic and socialist objectives.

One can approach this problem from a variety of different starting points. At the level of trade union response, the communist-socialist federation of Italian unions, CGIL, has chosen a new path by confining its international affiliations to the European trade union movement, severing its relationship with the Soviet-dominated World Federation of Trade Unions. This body is irrelevant to the needs of autonomous trade unions. At the level of electoral presence, the French Socialists and Communist Parties reached an entirely rational agreement on the principle of a Common Programme, whatever difficulties subsequently emerged. Yet at a more profound level, the actions of eurocommunists in defending the Prague Spring, or in resisting repressions inside the USSR, establish a prospect of moral consensus, which alone can make the possibility of joint action into something more vital than a limited contract. Up to now, on issues like that of the defence of Chilean socialists, communist-socialist actions on a European scale have been more parallel than joint.

But no-one can tackle the problem of building an opposition to re-armament, or unemployment, purely on the trade union level, or at the level of electoral pacts within particular nations: these world-wide issues require a general, inclusive, increasingly integrated response.

Those parties which have been loosening their ties with Moscow have made some important initial moves. Shall we see a fitting answering response from all the others? If the communists can take a genuine distance from the moribund politics of Moscow, can they not be met by autonomous socialists, themselves free of all taints of CIA patrimony?

Chapter 11

Power and the Party

Keith Middlemas has won general acclaim for his recent panorama of the British political system, in its development since 1911. Now he has produced another large and comprehensive study,* this time on West European communism, or to be more exact, on the four most important communist parties in Western Europe. Middlemas is the kind of writer whose insights bite even when they provoke disagreement. He also has a large capacity to reduce complex and opaque historical processes to convincing, logical narrative, so his book will be, as it deserves to be, very widely read.

Power and the Party rightly begins with two long historical essays setting the context of Western communism. The first provides a convenient short account of the Comintern, while the second documents the war-time and post-war experience of communism in Eastern and Central Europe. These years were dominated by the excommunication and subsequent public forgiveness of Tito, and their impact is nicely pin-pointed. Here we find Enver Hoxha, during a Tirana visit from Khrushchev, the purpose of which was discussion of Stalin's 'errors', admitting in 1959 that the dictator "made two mistakes. First, he died too early; and second, he failed to liquidate the entire present Soviet leadership". Then, in a welter of accusations after the repression of the Hungarian uprising of 1956, we have Tito, defending himself against the charge that it was impossible to build socialism on American wheat: "those who know how, can do it, while those who do not know how will not even be able to build socialism on their own wheat". At the end of the processes of adjustment and tension between the Soviet government and its East European allies lay the invasion of Prague in 1968. This

---

* Keith Middlemas: *Power and the Party — Changing Faces of Communism in Western Europe. André Deutsch, 1980.*

had profound effects on West European communism, because the Prague Spring had promised precisely the kind of pluralistic, democratic evolution as a practical choice towards which they had been converging as a theoretical option.

Middlemas summarises his view of the Soviet Union at the end of this period. "First", he says, "Westerners had divided as to whether the USSR was 'an aggressive revolutionary power' or 'an old-fashioned defensive one'." But as the Warsaw Pact crystallised, and as China became not merely independent but also hostile, so Eastern Europe assumed a "degree of economic and military integration that had barely existed in Stalin's day". "Russia", he goes on, "became an imperial and expansionist power (by the mid-1960s, a superpower)." There is some truth in this view, although two caveats are needed. First, with Chinese autonomy established beyond doubt, and having made sure, by severe provocations, of continuing and united Chinese mistrust, the Soviet authorities had to budget for defence on two fronts. This made for a mutation in their concept of 'defence', since this was no longer uni-directional, but complex. It is possible to explain (although not to justify) the recent invasion of Afghanistan in the light of this event. Second, whilst Soviet overseas commitments took on a truly global scale, and, in relation to, say, Ethiopia, began to reflect a more forward strategy than had hitherto been the case, nevertheless Soviet policy in relation to Europe remained hyper-cautious, conservative and, except in relation to fellow members of the Warsaw Treaty Organisation, pacific.

This becomes very clear when we follow Middlemas into the particular studies of his four chosen parties. These are the Communist Parties of France, Italy, Portugal and Spain. Much of the material featured in these chapters was gleaned from a long series of detailed interviews with leading members of the organisations concerned. There already exist several more or less informed accounts of eurocommunism, but this one is probably the most useful. Despite the odd literal mistake, the work reflects homework carefully done, and I, for one, found it very helpful to see material which had cluttered round odd corners in my head, here ordered in a tidily arranged sequence. I also found a lot of information which was new to me, some of it important.

The evidence of Russian concern not to bait the established

powers in Western Europe emerges very interestingly in the case of Portugal. The Portuguese, of course, are not in any conventional sense eurocommunists, and are commonly seen as the most Stalinist of the Western parties. But at the same time, they represent serious, and probably growing, support, and may well come to be seen again as a major force in Portuguese politics. Middlemas traces the story of the withdrawal of crucial Soviet support for the PCP, between the months of June and August 1975. Without such pressure, it is at least possible that Portuguese politics would have turned out differently. As things were, a combination of internal dissent and external pressure were sufficient to moderate the PCP's bid for control, which finally fell away during the last crisis of the Armed Forces' Movement, in the autumn of 1975.

At the moment the PCP is winning votes, while the PCI is fighting hard not to lose, and the PCF is losing. But all three organisations, and the Spanish Party as well, have a certain interdependence, even across the boundaries of their loyalties to the USSR (or their distances, for that matter). For instance, the departure of the PCF from the Union of the Left was a major blow to the PCP, which needs all the help it can get to reach accord with the larger Socialist Party alongside which it is a contender. In integral politics such shifts and starts weigh more heavily in Lisbon than does the French Party's dalliance with Russian civil liberties, or its rehabilitation of Bukharin. All parties which command any significant part of the popular vote, or any major working class, trade union following, must naturally comport themselves within the democratic culture of which they are a part, and failure to do so will result in a punishing loss of support. Yet external commentators frequently glide over such imperatives, and examine only the diplomatic communiques which reflect (usually very imprecisely) the international policies of the contenders. Middlemas avoids this pitfall.

At the same time, he makes it clear that, although the Russians were quite willing to use whatever forces they could command in order to lever support for their reassertion of control over Czechoslovakia, their direct intervention in the politics of Italian, French or Spanish eurocommunism has been confined to sustaining their doctrine on such issues within their sphere of influence. This does not mean that Soviet politics have not had their influence on the domestic policies of Western States. On the contrary, such influence has often been exercised to the detriment of 'fraternal' parties, as when the Soviet authorities have triggered unhelpful diplomatic events during election campaigns (France 1974), or received their political opponents in Moscow, with pomp. What is doubtful, however, is whether the Soviet government has any real objection to 'historical compromises' and the like, as long as they are unsuccessful. It would, however, be extremely inconvenient if they won, and even more so if they accomplished anything, because this would rock the boat. Unrest would suddenly find a focus, both Westwards and Eastwards. Law and order would be harder to maintain in Warsaw, as well as Paris. "Eurocommunism might actually be dangerous to *both* sides'', says Middlemas, echoing the Sonnenfeld doctrine, under which the Americans are to accept Soviet hegemony on their own sphere, in return for similar reciprocal courtesies.

How 'autonomous', then, will eurocommunism prove to be? It is hard to say. It depends on how long Western socialists insist on kicking gift horses in the teeth. The need of the hour, of the decade, and of the rest of the century, is that that European working class movement should find ways to converge upon its own goals, without benefit of intervention by the CIA, the KGB or any of their proteges. As national communisms in power become more and more embroiled in a mess of conflicting State interests, so the overlap of interest between 'communist' States and working class movements in the capitalist world becomes ever more coincidental. European workers need a common focus on disarmament and peace, on inflation and monetarism, and on the giant companies which exploit them. To aspire to this, they need to discover and pursue their own interests, unrefracted by State-crystallised ideologies. What is left of right-wing social democracy is collapsing back on its base of NATO funding, and what is left of pure-bred Stalinism is ever more openly exposed in suck on a Russian teat. It is time for a new beginning, linking the forces that are willing and able to act autonomously.

This book was prepared with no such end in view, but it will undoubtedly help all those who are seeking precisely that basis for a fresh start.

Chapter 12

Eurocommunism in the East

Ten years have elapsed since the extraordinary upsurge of May 1968 in France: and since the military restoration of Winter in Czechoslovakia. In that period of time there has been a prodigious growth of socialist commitment, throughout the West, whichever of a variety of measures be chosen to evaluate it.

In terms of electoral support the parties of the French Left, for all their disharmony, came within an inch of victory at the last poll, and have been improving their support ever since. The Italian communists gathered greater support at the last General Election than ever before in their history. The British Labour Party has maintained a marginal lead over its opponents for more of this time than not. Far more significantly, the fall of fascism and authoritarianism in Portugal, Spain and Greece has liberated and legitimised a prodigious socialist movement. Meanwhile, in all the Left parties which have been involved in governments, including the German Social Democratic Party, there have developed extensive discussions on the relevance of specifically socialist projects.

If we monitor, instead of the votes cast for mass parties standing to the left of centre, the proliferation of organised groups and schools of thought, or the growth of socialist publishing, we find a virtual explosion of concern and interest in every single West European country. Whole libraries would be needed to house the journals, newspapers and printed ephemera which have been engendered in each of these nations.

At the same time, the development of social crisis throughout the capitalist world maintains a continuous pressure upon the working class organisations which ensures that socialist prescriptions will have continuing relevance and even urgency. Unprecedented post-war levels of unemployment; continuing concentration of economic power in the hands of multi-national

corporations which undermine the writ of national laws; growing social malaise in disintegrating city centres, declining regions
and the areas dominated by dying industries; and a rising crisis
in welfare, health and environmental provision: all these trends
have combined to falsify the liberal perspectives which became
orthodox within the main social democratic parties during the
peak years of the long post-war boom. In 1956 in Britain, whilst
the small Communist Party was digesting the implications of the
20th Congress of the Soviet Communist Party, the young
aspirants to office in the Labour Party were reading and pro-
pagating C.A.R. Crosland's then all-dominating textbook on
The Future of Socialism. Seldom, it must be said, has an orthodoxy disappeared so completely, leaving so little behind. The
assumptions that the epoch of full employment had been
definitely established, that the fundamental structural crises of
capitalism were henceforward under the complete control of
Keynesian management policies, and that worker alienation was
really a problem of adjustment to 'the technological imperatives' all seem more dated, and more incomprehensible,
than the historic panaceas of Feargus O'Connor or Robert
Owen. Since 1968 we have all entered a different epoch.

How different are matters in the East? The barometer of
universal suffrage does not operate in a manner enabling us to
evaluate any shifts of opinion. Established governing parties
have, with some exceptions, been frozen in a doctrinal mould
which has resulted in the shivering official closure of the discussion which opened so hopefully in 1956. The result has been a
phenomenal growth of dissidence, some of which is undoubtedly
hostile to any form of socialism. In the USSR, two currents of
opposition have attracted the most widespread attention in the
West. The first of these emphasises, above all, personal
resistance, and fuses with a deep-rooted religious antagonism,
not only to the terrible excesses of Stalinism, but to the very notion of socialism, which it equates with rationalism and
godlessness. The second 'scientific' and liberal school of dissent
seeks to secure a variety of reforms which would give modern
Russia some of the advantages of liberal democracy. Broadly,
and over-simply, these trends could be ascribed to Solzhenitsyn
and Sakharov respectively. Both have, it seems, increasingly
despaired of winning support from their countrymen on a scale
adequate to form a new public opinion, and have therefore

devoted more and more of their energies to the mobilisation of external international pressures upon the Russian government.

By contrast, there exists a specifically socialist opposition. The most consistent spokesmen of this have been the brothers Zhores and Roy Medvedev, who seek to finds ways of realising the humane and democratic promise within communism, so that they therefore search out every possible means of persuasion within the given (undeniably restrictive) framework of Soviet political organisation. This commitment means that they behave differently from other dissidents. Instead of calling upon American senators to hot up the cold war, they urge more and faster progress towards detente, greater trade and intensified cultural and scientific contact. Not seeing the capitalist democracies as a force necessarily standing on their side, they are compelled to appeal for such support as they require to their own fellow-citizens, and to seek ways of encouraging discussion among them.

Of course, this means that their first appeal is to 'intellectuals'. The near-total official discouragement of original and independent political thought which has been a feature of Soviet society for so long has not only strongly inhibited free ranging public discussion of any kind, but it has also brought about a prolonged freeze upon all autonomous working class initiatives. It is instructive to watch how the Medvedevs have been compelled to circle the political field in order to discover ways of opening up the argument. On the one side, Roy Medvedev has mounted his frontal attack, in his epic history of Stalinism, *Let History Judge,** and in his extended programmatic manifesto, *On Socialist Democracy.*** It could be said that the joint account of the Khrushchev years (which was published during 1977 under the names of both the brothers) is a continuation of this offensive.

On the other side, there are the special issue-centred campaigns, in which some notable abuse is identified, isolated and brought under a laser beam of accurately deadly criticism. Since, where there exists centralised hierarchy, public issues are invariably tied to the dominance of particular personalities, this commonly means the exposure of a specialised dictatorship, like that which began the international reputation of Zhores

* Spokesman, 1976.
** Spokesman, 1977

Medvedev. His painstaking account of the rise of Trofim D. Lysenko, Stalin's quack geneticist, documented not only the unscientific methods of that imposter, but also laid bare the whole scarifying story of the elimination of those who had been his opponents in the schools of genetics, such as Academician Vavilov.*

At one level, this book showed how the dictatorship had trodden down all the most promising Soviet geneticists, and all possibility of scientific work in their fields. But at another level, it began an intense political discussion among Soviet scientists, within which debate they could press forward all the wider arguments which so obviously leap to mind, once argument becomes at all seriously possible. In the event, Zhores' book was considered for publication by the Academy of Sciences, and once their decision had been over-ruled by the censorship, the number of persons who had read the book and become directly involved in the argument had already become significant. In modern Russia, failure to secure permission to publish a work sometimes seems to be a precondition for its success. Be that as it may, Lysenko was a symbol for a whole legion of anti-scientific practices, and once his methods were openly opposed and denounced even on the restricted plane of his own field of study, the metaphor spelt out in his unedifying story could be read by everyone who cared to look anywhere else across the entire spectrum of political life. After all, the impetus to burn scientific witches had not arisen in any biochemists' laboratories: Lysenko had risen to his ugly prominence entirely as a result of political decisions.

Roy Medvedev has since begun within the field of literature the same kind of bulldozing moral clearance which was earlier accomplished by his brother in the scientific domain. The Soviet Writers' Union, not in its stolid majority a notably progressive (nor yet liberal) body, set up, during 1974, an anniversary committee to celebrate the 70th birthday of Mikhail Sholokhov. The earliest work of this author to obtain a wide audience had been *The Quiet Don,* which deservedly gained a Nobel Prize in 1970. More recent published utterances of Mr Sholokhov have not taken the form of novels or stories, but that of somewhat

* *The Rise and Fall of T.D. Lysenko.* Columbia UP, 1969
** *Problems in the Literary Biography of Michael Sholstov.* Cambridge UP, 1977.

obscurantist political statements. No-one could claim that Sholokhov was a fraud in the Lysenkoan mode, without any claim to be considered seriously. There is no doubt that Sholokhov has written readably upon a number of occasions. However, there is considerable doubt that *The Quiet Don* was one of these: for more and more evidence comes to light to suggest that this acknowledged masterpiece might be one of the greatest plagiaries of our epoch, and that, if this were true, Sholokhov would be seen as something worse than a literary Van Meegeren, who after all, did imitate the old masters for himself. Sholokhov, by contrast, stands accused of having abstracted either much or most of his own most distinguished work from that of some other writer. The most likely candidate for the true authorship, if this case is established, is Fyodor Kryukov, who died in 1920 after living and fighting through all the events described in the earlier books of *The Quiet Don.*

The argument about this matter is not a new one. Long before the *Times Literary Supplement* opened fire on the question in the middle 'seventies, when Solzhenitsyn and the Soviet literary critic known as 'D' offered their opinions on these questions, there were, as Medvedev claims early in his book "endless variations of the legend that tells us how Sholokhov apparently found the manuscript of an unfinished novel in the map case of a Cossack officer who had died . . .''. As long ago as 1929 a commission of the Moscow State Publishing House had been set to work 'to examine the accusations brought against Sholokhov'. Although this ruled for Sholokhov, it seems that many Soviet writers remained unsatisfied. Their names include Novikov-Priboy, Gorbatov, and possibly Gorky, who adjudged the whole business to be 'strange' after he had been introduced to the then youthful and monosyllabic Sholokhov. But it was only in the late 'thirties that the posthumous claims of Kryukov began to be asserted in (unpublished) letters to the press. Some authors of such letters were arrested.

Roy Medvedev chronicles this story in some detail, but his book does far more. In a series of forensic arguments, he asks what are the hallmarks of *The Quiet Don,* considered as if it had been anonymous: and then, what measures of 'fit' with these hallmarks can be offered by the respective authorship claims of Sholokhov himself, and of Kryukov. As a piece of literary detective work, these chapters make quite fascinating reading. After a review of the evidence, which is a model of objective argument, Medvedev permits himself a judgment which most of his readers will have come to share:

> Every Russian winner of the Nobel Prize has been treated unkindly by fate. The first of our compatriots to win (it) was Ivan Bunin, who had emigrated . . . the second was Boris Pasternak who was subjected after the Award to torment and persecution sufficient to make him officially renounce the Prize . . . Solzhenitsyn had been forcibly expelled . . . Finally, Mikhail Sholokhov has had to spend all his life defending himself against charges of plagiarism.''

But why should such an eminently political thinker concern himself about such problems? Do questions of authors' copyright have any real implications for the study or reform of the political economy of the USSR? Most decidedly they do. Free discussion on such matters would clearly embarrass a significant part of the cultural establishment, which is knitted integrally with the political elite. This explains why it is resisted. It is not possible to recreate cultural politics without reopening political arguments across the entire range of social issues.

The need for free discussion could never be more cogently established than in the tragi-comic, hopeful and despairing tale of Khrushchev's rise and fall.

In their joint assessment of Khrushchev,* the Medvedevs are in part assessing their own aspirations and disappointments: Roy's potted biography, taken from one of his publisher's blurbs, tells us that he joined the CPSU in 1956, after the 20th Congress; while this extraordinary book shows how, from hopefully attacking 'the cult of personality' Khrushchev evolved into a position of such authority that his most eccentric whims became laws and plans rolled into one. Khrushchev's disastrous agricultural policy is documented with lethal effect. One chapter, 'Fiasco in Riazan Oblast', shows how authoritarian 'planning' totally devastated farming over a wide and rich area. It will be featured in all forthcoming anthologies on 'How Not to Plan'.

The development of this kind of samizdat literature is not anchored on the hope of publication in the West, although it may indeed benefit from being reflected back into the intellectual life of the Soviet Union from outside. But the fact that this kind of discussion is becoming possible, if only in clandestine condi-

---

*   Khrushchev: The Years in Power. Oxford UP, 1977.

tions, signals the ultimate rebirth of powerful democratic pressures.

What might be called the 'loyal' opposition within the States of the Comecon block now reaches over a very wide area indeed. Scholars like Hegedus from Hungary, Havemann from the German Democratic Republic, the Charter supporters from Czechoslovakia, represent widely different strategic prescriptions for change, but at the same time constitute the core of a genuinely democratic argument in the modern conditions, and in the given received historic legacies, of these societies.

But the argument about socialism cannot be confined to democratisation, indispensible though this is. This is understood, and powerfully highlighted, in Rudolf Bahro's recent book, *The Alternative*,* which makes a crucially important point.

Socialism is, and always has been, about the abolition of the division of labour in society, although every generation forgets the fact, and it is the easiest thing in the world to settle for something less. Those we call opportunists are prone to settle for the amelioration of its worst effects upon the groups they represent, or on themselves: while stern dogmatists settle instead for a devaluation of the task itself, turning it into a lesser matter such as nationalisation of the means of alienated production, or the dictatorship of a disembodied proletariat.

Because, in all sobriety, the overcoming of the fragmentation of people in mutilating and stultifying economic roles is a task for a long haul, life seems to become simpler if the whole process is indefinitely postponed. Left-wing political parties in capitalist democracies tend to relegate it to a largely forgotten maximum programme, to which reference is occasionally made on May Day. Working days can then proceed undisturbed by uncomfortable thoughts of a new moral world. Governments are even tougher, and even more amnesiac. In all the self-proclaimed 'socialist' societies, postponement has been the rule. (True, in Yugoslavia self-management reserves an important claim on our attention, and in China, while Reds were more valued than experts, there might have been at least a chance of thinking about the problem). In general, the State Socialist governments have incorporated workers' trade union organisations in the pursuit

* New Left Books, 1978.

of productivity, have intensified supervision and Taylorist organisational principles in the factories to an unprecedented degree, have elevated the stopwatch far above creative initiative as a motor of industrial activity, and have driven the subdivision of mental labour within their ramified bureaucracies to a point approaching folly.

While the founding fathers of socialism spoke of a world in which the 'free development of each is a condition for the free development of all' and looked forward to a State in which men would 'hunt in the morning, fish in the afternoon, and critically criticise in the evening', the current 'socialist' reality is a vast pyramid of occupational ranks fortified by formal qualifications in separate technical compartments, resting on a minutely organised division of routine tasks, often involving ruthless piecework and always resting on externally imposed norms. Lenin, in a dreadful moment of technocracy, spoke of organising the whole of Soviet society as if it were a single factory: and his official inheritors have taken him, literally and starkly, at his word. For Marx, free time was 'the most creative time of all'. For official Marxism, so rigorously external is work discipline that leisure itself becomes an activity not in the slightest degree less alienated than compulsory labour. We need hardly add that, in the outside world of late capitalism, things are in no way easier.

It is upon this broad realisation that Rudolf Bahro bases his magnificent work. Without the least exaggeration, and without any necessity to endorse all its arguments, it is absolutely clear that this is the most important book on socialist theory to have appeared anywhere in the world since the Second World War. "The devil is not generally to be found in details," he tell us: and while his book contains all the detail it needs, its astounding merit is that it sustains, throughout its length, an overall perspective which is resonantly humanist, yet dispassionate and vast. Small wonder that the brutal little men in power in East Berlin have found it necessary to lock this author away. Eight years in prison, however, will not be sufficient to cancel his message, which will still present a powerful and necessary challenge even a hundred years from now. Perhaps the remarkable thing about Karl Marx is the fact that his fundamental ideas continually bring on this degree of fierce repression: it seems clear that the old sage will never be outdated until all the world's reactionaries, including those who call themselves 'Marxists' no longer need to put him safely behind bars. Bahro's great merit is unquestionably derived in considerable measure from his close fidelity to the beliefs of Marx: to the morality of the Economic and Philosophical Manuscripts of 1844, and to the analysis of the *Grundrisse*. It is also derived from a totally extraordinary open-mindedness and lack of rancour, which has to be carefully read to be believed.

Bahro is concerned to apply Marxian categories to the better understanding of what he calls "actually existing socialism", which "is a fundamentally different social organisation from that outlined in Marx's socialist theory". He rejects theories of deformation, according to which a variety of different sins of omission by revolutionary leaders are to a greater or lesser extent responsible for the progressive degeneration of initially pure socialist forms of society. More fundamental than these short-comings, he tells us, is the social structural inheritance of the young Russian Soviet society, which was marked by the key characteristics of what Marx had styled the 'Asiatic' mode of production. In itself, this argument is not new, and it will always be associated with Karl Wittfogel, the former communist author of *Oriental Despotism*. But Bahro does not follow Wittfogel into the excesses of his position, and offers an original and fresh statement of this case, which carries weight. While Wittfogel, in his later work, abstracted from various antique irrigation-based despotisms a whole series of unpleasant features which could then be randomly (and not without malice) attributed to modern Russia, Bahro is concerned to assess the inherited influence of the material division of labour in Asiatic society, and his account therefore remains explicative rather than propagandistic. Indeed, searchers after propaganda will generally find this whole work disappointing: it is calm, and so secure in its heresies that they require a very minimum of overt moral indignation.

If the Soviet inheritance from Asiatic forms of organisation is truly considerable, more contentious is Bahro's assessment of the passivity of the working class in 'actually existing socialism''. Unlike the shop stewards at Lucas Aerospace, or legions of other Western socialist innovators whose social origins are purely proletarian, East European workers are denied all independent forms of organisation and representation, and the result is that they are relatively atomised or, in a more familiar Western jargon, privatised. What does this fact spell in the language of political change? Bahro thinks in terms of a built-in capacity which, he believes, inhibits workers from the spontaneous pursuit of socialist goals, and he tends to extrapolate this observation from East Germany (where it does, at any rate for the moment, seem to hold good) to the Western capitalist powers (where it seems very wide of the mark indeed). Yet nothing in this argument is simple, and it requires careful and deliberate consideration.

For the alternative which is needed in his zone of the world, to reopen the Marxian crusade against the division of labour, Bahro uses the metaphor of the cultural revolution. This has its problems, since it is associated with historical events rather far removed from the kind of programme Bahro has in mind. But for any reader willing to work behind the verbal formulae of this rich book, to its underlying concepts, Bahro's prescription is not only new, but unique and profoundly exciting.

*   *   *

The two levels of oppositional socialist activity in the East are well represented in these examples. On the one hand, the critique of institutions on the basis of democratic criteria: on the other, the critique of official devaluation of the long-term objectives of the socialist movement. It is by no means necessary to postulate either complete correspondence, or for that matter, complete divergence, between the implications of these critiques. Logically, a variety of juxtapositions between the results of the two levels of argument are perhaps equally likely. In practice, the classic Marxian project rests on the assumption that Bahro's goals may be best approached by Medvedev's methods. But the possible discrepancy between the two exists and is real. A key component of authoritarian trends in socialism is based upon the plea that democratic means must be suspended in order the more rapidly to approach the ultimate goal. This has provoked recurrent reactions along the lines frequently (and to some extent unjustly) attributed to Bernstein: 'the movement is everything, the goal is nothing'. Such reactions are unhelpful, since even the most restrictive and narrow minded democracy depends, for its legitimacy, on the capacity of at least a part of its constituency to relate to utopian perspectives. When

Kolakowski tells us that all attempts at socialism are in fact attempts to make gods of men, and therefore doomed to fail, he is taking up the same position as a whole chain of converts from the Left: not only in offering a metaphor which obscures more than it reveals, but also in sundering the democratic practices which he admires from the broad social aspirations outside which they could never be nurtured.

Bahro's assault upon the division of labour is not merely a doctrinal response to bureaucratisation and institutional hierarchy: it is also an incitement to greater equality and wider democratic involvement. Medvedev's onslaught on censorship, legal and political arbitrariness, and administrative repression may indeed make sense in its own right, but it makes far greater sense as part of the pursuit of a society in which the 'free development of each is the condition for the free development of all'.

It should be obvious that these considerations have their own direct relevance in the West also. First, in terms of the strategy of socialist movements, there is the need to fix a relation between day-to-day programmes and ultimate objectives which can not only inspire and maintain the momentum for far-reaching change, but also develop an expanding democratic base. Virtually the entire European Left is now beginning to converge on this type of programme, seeing the transition to socialism in terms of wider and deeper struggles to maintain and drive forward democratic processes into every corner of industry and society. To the extent that we can do this, we can overcome the old disjunction between minimum and maximum programmes, which means that socialist forms of organisation were never relevant in practice, while theory had little or nothing to do with any measure for which actual struggles might be co-ordinated.

Second, in terms of exemplary force, we must recognise not only the negative example of Bahro's 'actually existing socialism' throughout Western Labour Movements, but also the powerful positive inspiration of the Prague Spring, which risked making socialism popular, not only in Czechoslovakia, but also in England, Italy or France. No doubt that is why it seems so easy for vast troop movements to take place without any apparent disturbance of the diplomatic relations between the great powers: if Sonnenfeldt had never existed, he would quickly have been invented.

Thirdly, we must recall that Spring began to show its face in the Central Committee of the Czechoslovak Communist Party, whatever the climatic and seismic changes which surrounded that body. That is to say, the mass of socially conscious and active people in the East who identify with official communist parties may well include many arrivistes and more greedy careerists, but it also includes millions of potential readers of Bahro and the Medvedevs. In this context, it would be absurd to ignore the fact that, for all who read official scripture, there are resonant attacks by Marx *and* Lenin on censorship: that democratic subversion of autocracy is not on the agenda for the first time in this century of turmoil. Whatever 'Leninism' may mean as a body of doctrine, Lenin's writings remain full of arguments which are inconvenient, in the highest degree, for authority.

And associated with this, we must face the overwhelming fact of the world's balance of terror, in which our Western economic crisis is liable, as so often before, to provoke renewed speed-up in an already dizzy arms race. The effect of this, were it to develop unhindered by popular protest, would be to rigidify the Eastern bureaucracies, and brake the widening social pressure for reform. This would inhibit necessary change both in the East *and* West. For those who seek a marriage between socialism and liberty, the first task is, beyond doubt, the pursuit of wider international unity, overcoming old divisions, and challenging both the mass unemployment which capitalism has inflicted on our peoples and the threats of rearmament which it once again begins to imply. If socialists and eurocommunists could move in this direction, they would gain more than increased autonomy and popular response. They might begin to create a political situation in which the choices were no longer structured around labels attached to dead heroes or villains, but crystallised around the living issues which we need to face.

Chapter 13

Ol' Man River

A couple of decades ago now, I got into trouble with the Labour Party's national offices on account of a Polish Professor called Leszek Kolakowski. I had recently become editor of the Labour student newspaper *Clarion*. One of the first things I did was to reprint a piece from Kolakowski called *What is Socialism?* It was an angry and savagely witty piece, but the moguls at Transport House were not upset by anything particular it said. They were cross because I had lifted it from Peter Fryer's *Newsletter,* which proved beyond any doubt whatever, that it was up to no good. Peter Fryer had been the *Daily Worker's* special correspondent in Hungary during the 1956 uprising, and he had resigned because his reports had been suppressed. *The Newsletter* was a slender broadsheet which he edited during a brief flirtation with English Trotskyites, who were a thorn in the side of the Labour Establishment. Threats were made: perhaps our subsidy might be cut. Fortunately, other more serviceable witches presented themselves on stage at this point in the dialogue, and my interrogators were compelled to switch their attention from the universities in order to settle the hash of some other dissidents in the Party at large. By the time this dreadful (if miniscule) menace had been averted at the cost of much official excitement and a great deal of incomprehension in the ranks, everybody at Transport House had forgotten all about academics in general, to say nothing of Professor Kolakowski in particular.

When Kolakowski's last book on Marxism* finally came off the presses of Oxford Univerity, however, the Labour Party's weekly newspaper asked me to review it. This, I fear, is the

---

* *Main Currents of Marxism: Its Rise, Growth and Dissolution* by Leszek Kolakowski. Vol. I: *The Founders:* Vol. II: *The Golden Age;* Vol. III: *The Breakdown*. Clarendon Press: Oxford University Press, 1978.

measure of the growth of my respectability over the intervening twenty years: the equivalent measure of Professor Kolakowski's is that he has finished the last two of its three volumes as a fellow of All Souls. This is not bad for one who once produced a newspaper which became famous because it published a picture under the title 'The Pope's Wife'.

Professor Kolakowski's theme concerns Marx and all his subsidiary isms. Volume One considers *The Founders,* and is perhaps the most interesting. Volume Two, the *Golden Age,* deals with the thought of the second international, and includes sections on Kautsky, Luxemburg, Bernstein, the Austro-Marxists and Sorel. The third volume he calls *The Breakdown,* presumably because this was the point at which the author lost any semblance of control over his material. It rockets through a chapter on Stalinism, a quick travesty of Trotsky, short sections on various more or less appealing academic figures or schools, and a few pages of after-thoughts on Mao Tse-Tung to conclude that Marxism "has been the the greatest fantasy of our century".

Kolakowski starts his book with the truism "Karl Marx was a German Philosopher", but although he pays more attention to philosophy than other matters, he does not in the least restrict his canvas to the impact of Marxism in that field. Rather he seeks to philosophise about the impact of Marxism on practically everything.

Occasionally he pauses, as when confronted by the writings of Adorno on music, and disclaims the competence to tread further. Such refreshing lapses in encyclopaedic pretension are few, however. Yet Kolakowski, although a man of very wide reading, is not sufficiently at home in some important fields to be able to do full justice to all-Marxism-in-the-round. On economics the book is not as strong as it could be, and the weakness becomes more pronounced as the work wears on. Sraffa, for instance, is not once mentioned, yet in the field of Marxian economics that name might easily have an importance over the next thirty years which could surpass the vast importance of Lukacs in the intellectual history of Marxism during the last few decades. On all questions of imperialism there is an empty space, since it seems that Kolakowski regards the third world as a place of outer darkness.

English socialist readers will find that Kolakowski knows as much about us as we knew about Polish socialism before we got this book. Guild socialism, for instance, was not as he believes, a 19th but very much a 20th century phenomenon, and, contrary to his judgment, it derived a considerable impetus from variant forms of Marxism. Not only that: itself it contributed largely to the fledgling communist movement, and among those it nurtured was the unspeakable R.P. Dutt, later to become arch-druid of the Stalin cult in Britain. Other things about Britain Kolakowski knows but doesn't say: in his onslaught on the New Left (which in its vulgarity, its capacity for amalgamating the separate views of contending tendencies, and its blithe rejection of any standards of fair discussion, is fully worthy of his own persecutors in Poland) he never mentions the work of Raymond Williams or E.P. Thompson.

But all these matters are quibbles. What is really wrong with Kolakowski's book is that at root it identifies utopian strivings in themselves as a key source of totalitarianism: which is contrary to what he himself used to believe, and is about as helpful as claiming the Sermon on the Mount as the source of the Holy Inquisition. True, if the code of loving gentleness had never been uttered, no-one could have infringed it. Equally true, villains always look for a noble flag to wrap themselves in when they set about their work, and Inquisitors more so than most. But the main 'utopian' component of socialism, the rejection of the humiliating industrial division of labour, which we are bound to take to be a fundamental task of Marxism, has also been an inspiration of every other humane trend of thought to emerge under modern capitalism. De Tocqueville will show Kolakowski why this division undermines Democracy in America, and Ruskin can explain why it thwarted art in England. More important, all the good people who won't ever hear about this book, or about any of the books it concerns, because they are toiling and moiling in mills and factories, mines and offices, will still need to keep at least a small anchor on the utopias Kolakowski rejects, if any atom of their social power is to be useable to retain for us any of that wide range of limited freedoms which he ardently wishes to uphold. Separations of powers, jury trials, free speech and publishing, and all the other Goods our author will now admit, were all mightily advanced in this country by working people who not merely had messianic deviations, but who often actually sang in the Messiah annually. "Every valley shall be exalted" they chanted, and they believed. Nothing such people ever did was chosen piecemeal: they couldn't even open a co-operative food shop without believing it to be the "first step on the road to the co-operative commonwealth."

No, we need the water from this stream, even though some people have put some of it to very impure uses.

You can begin to defend people against little injustices if there is a larger justice somewhere around, be it only at the back of your own mind. Our whole civilisation began to know that larger justice when Adam Smith told us, in its dawn years, that there was no difference between a porter and philosopher save in the use society had made of their talents. Most philosophers, East or West, do not advertise this heresy over-heartily, but non-philosophers need access to it nonetheless for that.

I doubt whether the new 'Pope's Wife' is ever going to get her picture in any of Leszek Kolakowski's forthcoming works: East European air is apparently good for dissident torch-bearers, since in all conscience it engenders enough of them: but torches flare badly in the misty Oxford climate, where they soon gutter and go out. When we finally get Rudolf Bahro out of *his* prison, I shall immediately launch a national fund to bribe the entire fraternity of Oxford scholars, at all costs, no expense spared, to keep him at a safe distance.

Chapter 14

Soviet Art and Science

I

Engineers of Human Souls

"The Soviet Writers' Congress", says the blurb of this account of the Writers' 1934 Congress,* "was the culmination of one of the richest periods of Soviet literary production . . ." This Congress, continues the anonymous contributor, "both summed up and closed the first momentous epoch and set the tone for the next".

In the years prior to 1934, Mayakovsky and Essenin had both committed suicide. In the years immediately after that date, between 1936 and 1939, Roy Medvedev speculated that maybe 600 writers, a third of the membership of the 'all-inclusive' union of Soviet writers formed at this Congress, were "arrested and destroyed". They included Boris Pilnyak, Isac Babel, Osip Mandelstam, Sergei Tretyakov, Kataev, and Bruno Jasiensky. Meyerhold was tortured to death, but numerous other theatre people simply disappeared. Justly does our contemporary blurb composer tell us about the "Soviet Union's profound impact" on "those interested in the development of literature in the struggle for socialism". Butchery does, after all, make a rather indelible impact. It was the best third who died. But nothing, it seems, makes any impact at all upon the editors who have reproduced these generally dismal texts verbatim, with no explanatory words, no commentary, no apology, only, at the end, a newly compiled index.

In 1934 there had been a temporary lull in the frenzy of repression which had accompanied collectivisation of the land, and it was widely hoped that the newly-founded Union of Writers would establish norms of cultural tolerance which might overcome the zealous persecutions of the earlier literary factions. In-

---

* *Soviet Writers' Congress 1934,* edited by H.G. Scott. Lawrence and Wishart, 1977.

stead, these ideological battles were to be nationalised and pushed through to the bloodiest of conclusions. This book reports
various speeches mainly by Zhdanov, Gorky, Radek and
Bukharin.

Zhdanov was a mental policeman who had the singular genius
of his profession to the highest degree. He had an unerring and
persistent eye for talent and honesty, against which he brought
to play every imaginable weapon in the arsenal of a profoundly
vicious State. In his sick contribution to this book this genius has
only just begun to reveal itself, and he still permits himself to
show us what he thinks of as his ideal. Writers, he tell us, are "in
comrade Stalin's words, engineers of the human soul". The
crass mechanism of the notion could be a parody, but it is not.
Zhdanov died in strange circumstances, and his alleged murder
was to become a key datum for the 'doctor's plot' which Stalin
was stewing up towards the end of his life. Before this event,
Zhdanov managed to persecute more artists, more lethally, than
any inquisition. His victims included Zoshchenko, Akhmatova,
Pasternak, Shostakovitch, Prokoviev, Eisenstein and
Grossman. Without the least reticence, he harassed all that was
best and most generous, most imaginative and intelligent. The
name of this harrassment was a beautiful example of
bureaucratic hypocrisy: it was called 'socialist realism'.

Gorky was a good middle-rank writer, and had been a notable
defender of civil liberty, in the earliest days of the Revolution.
His contribution to these proceedings is not very exciting, but
would certainly, at the time, have encouraged the hope for
greater tolerance. According to the Soviet authorities, Gorky
was to be murdered by police-chief Yagoda in 1936, while his
son had been similarly murdered in 1934, even at the moment
when the father was praising comrade Stalin in these sessions.

Bukharin, by far the most distinguished contributor to this
volume, was executed for his complicity in these murders
amongst others, if we were to believe the official record of his
trial. Of course, were are not to believe this record, since the trial
in question was a complete farrago, a gruesome witch-burning.
Previously, yet another contributor to this same volume, Radek,
had featured as prime victim in an earlier trial in which he, too,
had confessed to working for Hitler.

Radek in fact never worked for Hitler. He was a brilliant jour-
nalist, a man with all the vices of his chosen craft. What he knew

about literature was strictly comparable with what might be known by his English equivalents, working on *The Times*. Unfortunately, he didn't work on *The Times,* where he would have made an admirable forerunner for Bernard Levin, with different politics, but similar manners. He worked in the USSR, where his clever half-truths could become official 'reality', and his lazy vices could result in painful restrictions of the freedom of better men than himself. In his text here printed, he opens a scurrilous attack on James Joyce. Pressed to defend this (back in 1934 it was still possible to argue with an official ignoramus) he says:

"If a man writes a book of eight hundred pages without stops or commas, where all the parts are mixed up . . . this is something out of the ordinary." (And if, one might add, a man makes a speech of considerable length in which he says something like that, he proves that he has never opened, leave alone read, the works in question). That was how James Joyce was hunted out of the USSR.

But not quite. Eisenstein, the greatest of Soviet cinematographers, was a devoted disciple of *Ulysses.* Much of his pioneering development of montage would be, when people could speak freely again, unhesitatingly attributed to the influence of Joyce.

None of these principal protagonists of 1934 was allowed a natural death. What beliefs in more leisured cultures, might have been spoken calmly in a placid cultural debate, here grew teeth which ate the respective spokesmen.

When I was a young miner, I wrote to Sean O'Casey, then in his seventies, to ask him what he thought about 'socialist realism'. There has been a lot of blather about it, he replied, "without any who wrote about it having an idea of what it is or what it meant".

What it meant was repression, cynical invention, the promotion of greedy liars, and the birth of a new dissidence. This book, which began it all, opened one of the great tragedies of the 20th century, which throttled some of the noblest men and women of their time and destroyed the finest hopes of an entire generation. No wonder its publishers sneak it out, adding only an index, and keeping the blurb anonymous.

II

Dialectics and Alchemy

One of the pre-eminent men of the earliest days of Soviet Science

was N.I. Vavilov. At the beginning of the 'thirties there took place, in London, an international congress on scientific and technological history. A powerful delegation came from Russia, headed by Bukharin, who delivered a paper on Marxist theory. Hessen gave a remarkable lecture on the social and economic roots of Newton's *Principia,* which was reprinted all round the world, and which came to have an extraordinary influence on radical English scientists. And Vavilov submitted a brillant contribution on the origins of agriculture in the light of genetical research.

The impact of these and other Russian statements at that conference was soon to reach out far beyond the immediate concerns of their authors, and to become part of the cultural shock which created the red 'thirties, at least for a whole school of intellectuals. Two of these, J.D. Bernal and Maurice Cornforth, were, a decade and a bit later, to write a booklet on *Science for Peace and Socialism,* defending a very different 'scientific' tradition, with quotations from Stalin, Zhdanov and Lysenko. From opening ever new doors to enquiry, the Russian policy soon came to install a horrendous modern inquisition. Yet, between 1931 and 1948, not only the USSR, but the world-wide communist movement as well, including, as it did, hundreds of scientific workers, some of whom enjoyed celebrated reputations, all followed through from sharing in the thrill of the initial awakening of Soviet science to joining its acknowledgement and enthronement of witchcraft, not only without demur, but even with enthusiasm.

Proletarian Science? * is a book which sets itself the task of explaining this distressing episode. Its theme concerns the rise and fall of Trofim D. Lysenko, a vicious charlatan who 'purged' genetics of its most creative Soviet practitioners, including of course, N.I. Vavilov. At the time, Bernal and Cornforth rejoiced in this purge, showing with its long quotations from Engels, that Lysenko's reign of obscurantism was, really, all the time, the enlightenment itself. Of those who defended Vavilov, they said that they were "shouting about Galileo" in order to take the "side of the inquisition".

Distinguished (and not so distinguished) Marxist Frenchmen

---

*   *Proletarian Science? The Case of Lysenko* by Dominique Lecourt. New Left Books, 1977.

joined the same chorus, and it is the record of their reprehensible attitudes which has provoked Dominique Lecourt to offer what he wishes us to see as a 'Marxist analysis' of all this.

There is, of course, a definitive book on Lysenkoism already. It is the authoritative history by Zhores Medvedev, which Althusser, introducing Lecourt's book, tells us "cannot, in spite of its interest, be described as a *Marxist* history". Perhaps it can't, but it can be described as a *true* history, which is a good deal more than can be said of various self-proclaimed 'Marxist' works which are on offer. The rise of Lysenko was the extinction of Vavilov, but one can read Lecourt's book all the way through without ever being directly told what happened to Vavilov. On page 49 a footnote informs us, quite rightly, that "Medvedev . . . gives an excellent portrait of Vavilov, and a moving account of the conditions of his death". And that's all.

In fact, as Medvedev explains, Vavilov, after his arrest, was placed, in 1941, in a "windowless underground death cell. The condemned were even denied outdoor exercise . . . (later) Vavilov was moved to the general ward in a grave condition with symptoms of malnutrition. As he entered, he introduced himself: 'You see before you, talking of the past, the Academician Vavilov, but now, according to the opinion of the investigators, nothing but dung'. The prisoners treated Vavilov with great respect and later when . . . he could no longer walk, they would carry him outside, hoping that fresh air would give him some relief." In 1942 Vavilov was elected a member of the Royal Society. No one in London knew that the new FRS was expiring in Saratov Prison. Soon after, he died. Comparisons with Galileo, far from being otiose, are absolutely in order. But perhaps it may be remembered that even under ecclesiastical constraint Galileo was able to meet Hobbes, and that he succeeded in smuggling his major works out of confinement to be published in Holland.

The KGB, unlike the inquisition, was much more efficient in this respect. The apologists of the modern Holy Office, Cornforth and Bernal, and hundreds like them, were able for years to deny most strenuously that Vavilov's corpse was dead, and to assert that only bloodthirsty propagandists would accept that he had ever been in jail.

Lecourt thinks that Lysenko's triumph was 'consecrated' with the ascendency of a wrong-headed notion of 'proletarian science' derived from, if not at the time attributed to, the Russian philosopher Bogdanov. Perhaps this is arguable, but it seems to me not to be of primary interest in explaining what happened. The 1948 Congress on 'The Situation of Biological Science' was notable for a rearguard action in defence of genetics by P.M. Zhukovsky, which culminated in his dramatic capitulation, almost as if he were the accused at a show trial, at the end of the Session. Lecourt notices all this, but thinks that Zhukovsky's formal retraction of support for science in favour of rubbish was mediated by the erroneous theory of "two sciences", one alien and bourgeois, the other plebian and pure. I think this explanation is largely tommy-rot. Galileo was shown the instruments, and that was enough to persuade him to say what was wanted of him. Zhukovsky had no evidence whatever upon which to assume Lysenko to be right, even metaphorically. But he could, metaphorically, smell burning flesh, and that is a powerful argument, even in the most dispassionately conducted laboratories. Having looked again at the fantastic transcript of this frightful gathering, I am convinced that this is a perfectly adequate explanation of why Zhukovsky recanted. Like Galileo, again, he also lived to fight another day, if only posthumously. One of his students during these melancholy days was a young man called Zhores Medvedev.

Modern Marxism is a lot cleverer than Stalin's. Althusser, Colletti, Anderson, Mandel, a little legion of others, all give us ingenious and mutually contradictory accounts of how the body politic is glued together, and very stimulating they all are. With a pinch of salt, they may all do good. The 'Marxist' lesson of Lysenko, like the 'liberal' lesson, is perfectly simple: without that *Grano salis* all such exciting theories are deadly poison. A generation of bright young Western scientists were awoken to Vavilov's generous message of radical renewal in 1931, and subsequently they found themselves wandering into crass apologetics for his detractors, and direct lies about his own fate in 1942. They bear eloquent (if too often mute) witness to this important fact. Pass the cruet, please, Mr Lecourt.

Chapter 15

An End to Artificial Certainty?

Maurice Cornforth has not been my favourite author in the past, because he has always written in full canonicals, as a potent dignatory of the Muscovite confession.

This book* reveals an altogether more engaging thinker. In his preface, Cornforth offers a few autobiographical remarks and a number of political perceptions which prepare us for a different kind of work from those he has previously given us. In addition to Marx and Lenin, he cites *King Lear:*

"The weight of this sad time we must obey
Speak what we feel, not what we ought to say".

So what *does* a highly intelligent communist philosopher feel about a world in which Gulag has become undeniable, Prague has been Husaked back into sullen conformity, and the Soviet Union has become a superpower against which, he tells us, socialists "may have to find the means to protect themselves"? Well, he feels much like many of us, independent socialists, which means that all of us will disagree with him, but all taking issue on different things. When he asks his "gentle readers" for their "charity", he may be sure he will get it, because at least some of the time we get the impression that he is in the same kind of muddle as the rest of us. That makes it easy for us all to be kind to one another. But we still need to get out of the muddle.

Cornforth hopes to help us do this with a whole stack of new books, some of which are about to appear. They will range over questions of scientific method, logic, dialectics and the nature of values and value-judgments. Although his blurb tells us that "his *Dialectical Materialism* (in three volumes) has long been a

---

* *Maurice Cornforth: Communism and Philosophy.* Lawrence and Wishart, 1980.

standard introduction", his present text now informs us that dialectical materialism is metaphysical, and thus quite, quite un-Marxian. Of course, he is right.

Stuart Macintyre's very useful history of Marxism in Britain up to 1933* shows how the Soviet dogma of dialectical materialism was imported, neat, and how it clashed with the preconceptions of the old Marxists, trained in Labour Colleges on the m.c.h. (materialist conception of history) and the rather diffuse works of 'Ditchkin' (Joseph Dietzgen, the German worker/philosopher whose *Positive Outcome of Philosophy* was a basic text for a whole generation of self-taught British socialists). In fact it was Plekhanov who invented dialectical materialism, and the doctrine was subsequently codified to the point of incoherence, whereupon it became obligatory in Stalin's Russia. A lot of Russians were killed or imprisoned for real infractions, but some perished, or were long victimised, for nothing more than the reluctance to swallow all this. Deborin, a distinguished thinker, was denounced and witch-hunted for 'menshevising idealism", or, some thought, for preferring Marx's Marxism to the subsequent varieties. To the end of his days Deborin never found out what 'menshevising idealism' was.

The remarks which Maurice Cornforth makes about the doctrine are to the point. However, what is more interesting is the use to which it was put.

If the doctrine cannot elucidate real problems, obligatory adherence to it must serve to obfuscate them. Why does a State need such obfuscatory mechanisms? Marx and Engels in turn wrote interesting things on this matter. Rubbish is never neutral, if you get it into your head. That is why we must give one cheer to Maurice Cornforth for helping to clear it out. Two further cheers, however, we shall be wise to reserve to her or him who can explain who dumped it, and what for, and in whose interest. It certainly didn't serve the workers' cause. What it did was to blind the credulous with science, which makes it part of the art of manipulating a mass, not part of a work of liberation.

But I do not wish to damn this book with faint praise. I disagree with some of what it says, and I might well disagree

---

* Stuart Macintyre: *A Proletarian Science — Marxism in Britain, 1917-33.* Cambridge University Press, 1980.

with what its next and next but one volumes are going to say. None of this matters at all; what is important is the tone of voice in which Cornforth speaks, which reflects not a mannerism, but a series of hard-earned lessons, all of which make for discussion of a different kind, at a different level, from that of his earlier concordances. And it is in that appreciation that I think it most important to debate with Cornforth on his appreciation of nationalism and internationalism.

Rightly, he insists that there is no 'international working class' but a multiplicity of working classes situated in different nation States. I say rightly, but I should be more careful, because although classes define themselves in relation to national polities, transnational capitalism is beavering over, beneath and round those polities to lethal effect. Making due allowance for that fact, the crisis of socialist internationalism is not simply that trade unions cannot match and place Shell or Courtaulds on the relevant near-universal scale. No. National socialisms make war on one another. Spheres of influence rend not only the capitalist, but the emerging socialist, worlds. Caught between the blocs, the workers' movement finds no framework within which to crystallise a genuine internationalism. Without a relevant institutional focus, no internationalist potential will find room to develop. Today, the only functional alliances between unions or workers' parties are predominantly regional. This means that the quality of our response to urgent events is greatly feebler than it need be, if only we were prepared to worry at the problem.

Of course, a Comintern won't work, particularly when there might be two or three contending cominterns. And alas, the socialist international is woefully inadequate even for the limited tasks it sets itself: although such is the nature of national State pressures within it that perhaps this weakness is a blessing in disguise. But if socialists cannot converge upon new forms of international association, they will suffer more, and worse, setbacks than those which Cornforth honestly records. In communism there was no international force which was capable of confronting Stalin's terror: polycentrism, far from meeting this problem, has (in the circumstances, understandably) walked away from it. Now as a result there is no communist centre which could authoritatively adjudicate in the conflicts between socialist nations of different kinds. Neither is there a credible socialist centre which can organise solidarity with Bolivia, even though convergent efforts by workers throughout the world could put a mighty squeeze upon the the new junta. Chile yesterday, Bolivia today . . . yesterday Greece, Portugal, Spain, all working their way out of dictatorship . . . who knows who will need help tomorrow?

In the practice of Marx there are some clues about all this. If our practice can develop those clues, we may make conditions in which people can write more hopefully than Maurice Cornforth, without reverting to his earlier, now happily displaced, artificial certainties.

Stuart Macintyre's account of the intermingling of native British Marxisms with the official Russian scriptures is a valuable one. He shows how there developed among British working people a culture of self-discovery, which produced a generation of auto-didacts like T.A. Jackson and J.T. Murphy. In the most balanced account of the Labour Colleges which has yet appeared, he traces the impact of Soviet Marxism on British socialist thinking. For any who believe that the propensity to gull and be gulled is a purely Russian characteristic, this work is necessary. It chronicles all sorts of bizarre feuds which arose on native soil, and which reveal a domestic penchant for folly which is by no means inferior to any foreigner's. In 1928, seven Labour College students were expelled for failure to participate in the Dietzgen Centenary celebrations, for instance. Nonetheless, when the first graduates returned from Moscow's new Lenin School in 1928, we may be forgiven for thinking that their primary function was a bit more rudimentary than 'to raise the level of Marxist understanding' in the communist party. It was the end of the Tommy Jackson era, and the beginning of the age of the apparatchik. And it coincided with the rise of Harry Pollitt and R.P. Dutt. At the Congress in which all this was consummated, Ernie Cant, a steadfast militant of the old school, had with others to be voted off the Central Committee. With great verve, eager young Stalinist delegates subsequently sang the Internationale, laying much stress on the words:

"at last ends the age of Cant."

They were mistaken. Canting had a long run in front of it. There is always work for the bullshit dozer to do, and no doubt this will continue to be so.

Chapter 16

Peace, Jobs and Democracy

"At this moment, for example, in 1984 (if it was 1984), Oceania was at war with Eurasia and in alliance with Eastasia. In no public or private utterance was it ever admitted that the three powers had at any time been grouped along different lines. Actually, as Winston well knew, it was only four years since Oceania had been at war with Eastasia and in alliance with Eurasia. But that was merely a piece of furtive knowledge which he happened to possess because his memory was not satisfactorily under control. Officially the change of partners had never happened. Oceania had always been at war with Eurasia. The enemy of the moment always represented absolute evil, and it followed that any past or future agreement with him was impossible."

George Orwell was a bit premature. But the developments for which so many people hoped and worked, for so many years, which have first brought The People's Republic of China to its seats in the United Nations Organisation and its Security Council, and now at last restored diplomatic relations between the most populous nation in the world and the world's wealthiest metropolis, have not marked out the unambiguous progress towards detente and long-term peace which their advocates had wished to serve.

Instead, we now find ourselves on the brink of a three-way arms race, in which Oceania, Eastasia and Eurasia are very likely to become entrapped with even more destructive results than those which accompanied the old cold war which raged between two contenders.

When Britain furnishes jump jets to the Chinese, and the Soviet government issues prickly warnings to the British government (and also to the Italians), no-one should underestimate the necessary outcome. Whatever the rights and wrongs of the Sino-

141

Soviet border dispute, and the evidence is by no means all stacked against the Chinese, it is perfectly obvious that the Soviet military establishment will wish to reinforce that frontier, and will seek to augment its budgets accordingly. This will 'provoke', or more accurately, excuse, yet further increases in NATO allocations. Heaven knows, they are already heavy enough!

TABLE I

NATO Military Budgets 1978

	% GNP
USA	5.5
UK	4.9
France	3.9
West Germany	3.4*
Belgium	3.3
Netherlands	3.3
Portugal	3.3
Norway	3.1
Denmark	2.5
Italy	2.5
Canada	2.0

*4.2% if aid to Berlin included

In a sense, the fearful dimensions of this baleful evolution are liable to distract our attention from a number of equally serious issues. First, from the viewpoint of potential victims, 'conventional' warfare is rapidly taking on a horrific quality which has already far surpassed the man-made disasters of Hiroshima or Dresden.

On the day that we read in our newspaper that President Carter was 'proposing a freeze on social services spending' and an increase in 'the Pentagon budget, in *real* terms, by about 3 per cent* there was, on other pages, another graphic story, concerning a law-suit by the estate of a veteran of the Vietnam war, who had contracted cancer simply because he had handled

* That is to say, in monetary terms, by 10 per cent.

the defoliant 245-T, or 'agent orange'. The victim, Paul Reutersham, had died at the age of 28, from a particularly virulent cancer, having been one of the army of people involved in spraying 44 million pounds of agent orange over Indo-China. When the spraying stopped, two million surplus gallons of the material were deemed too dangerous to use for any other purpose. Vietnam drank all these poisons into its soil, but presumably has no claim on the US government. The late Mr Reutersham, however, left behind a claim for £10,000,000 against the Dow Chemical Company. The herbicides supplied by Dow were apparently heavily contaminated by dioxin, the chemical which was accidently discharged into the air of Seveso during 1976, causing such widespread damage and chaos.

The extent of the genetic damage which may be caused by these poisons is as yet not accurately known. Yet defoliants were seen by the military brass as a relatively innocuous part of the Vietnam war, at the time their use was challenged. For sure, the horrors in today's arsenals include far more sophisticated torments than those which killed Mr Reutersham and evacuated Seveso, however lethal their effects may be on unborn generations of Vietnamese farmers.

Secondly, even if war by accident could be excluded, rearmament remains the most hazardous of options for a world which is racked by acute crisis. As the developed capitalist countries slide into prolonged slump, unemployment, and particularly youth unemployment, has become an endemic disorder. 1978, alleged to be a year of 'recovery' in general economic terms, saw a 12 per cent increase in unemployment in 14 European countries (see Table II). If the young cannot be found civilian work, is it too far-fetched to think that a section of the ruling establishment in the Western countries may come to find a new appeal in the idea that the unwanted new generation might be put into uniform? In fact, while an uneasy peace has held the two dominant blocs apart ever since 1945, their military potential has always been a threat, not only to any possible foreign adversary, but also to domestic malcontents. In Britain, the extraordinary chorus which has opened 1979, in which there have been loud and insistent calls for a 'state of emergency' in order more openly to deploy the armed forces in circumventing the effects of strikes, is an ominous pointer to the possibilities of a new offensive against democratic rights and civil freedoms. In the East

TABLE II

Unemployment — Western Europe

	1978 Nos. '000	%	1977 Nos. '000	%
Austria	40	1.4	28	1.0
Belgium	353	10.4	273	9.3
Denmark	179	8.3	136	6.5
Finland	147	6.6	136	5.7
France	1,344	N/A	968	N/A
Germany (West)	902	3.9	931	4.1
Ireland	99	N/A	81	11.7
Italy	1,658	7.5	1,692	7.7
Netherlands	210	5.3	186	4.8
Norway	43	2.3	35	1.9
Spain	833	N/A	507	N/A
Sweden	89	2.1	62	1.5
United Kingdom	1,429	6.0	1,450	6.2
Yugoslavia	708	11.5	660	11.4
	8,034		7,145	

This represents a 12½ per cent increase for 1978 over 1977

Sources: Bulletin of Labour Statistics, ILO, 4th Quarter 1978.
Yearbook of Labour Statistics, ILO, 1977.

European experience, military forces have been primarily deployed against internal dissent, most notably in Czechoslovakia in 1968.

No doubt this explains why those East European nations with the most independent political leaderships have been profoundly concerned by the renewed pressures for rearmament. President Tito specifically warned against this danger, in his statement to the 1978 Congress of the League of Communists of Yugoslavia. Romania has very courageously declined to join a Warsaw Pact commitment to an increase in military spending calculated to match the latest round of increased NATO appropriations. The Poles, who did not reject this commitment out of hand, appear to be hastening very slowly to implement it.

What of the West European States? All of them have real social problems, in the wake of the slump. Not only does widespread unemployment produce obvious economic ill-effects, but it provokes community tensions, increases racial and minority disharmonies, and undermines democratic institutions, including trade unions and workers' organisations. Increased military commitments will offer no real solution to any of these problems: new military technology is, in any case, highly capital intensive, and very likely to reduce the necessary manning levels necessary to any particular process of barbarity. But more soldiers, more fears, more hysteria *are* well established, if unscrupulous, means of social control, which may well appeal to increasingly desperate leaders who lack any constructive alternative sense of direction.

Because we value our planet and do not wish to drift to war, because we value our liberties, and do not wish to be compelled to salute Big Brother in any new State of Oceania, and because forcible unemployment in a world which is strangling in unmet needs is an insult to the human imagination, we must surely begin to organise a suitable response, on a Pan-European scale, to these dreadful challenges. Peace, Jobs and Democracy should become the watchwords of young people all across Europe, and the platform of every honest Labour organisation. Can we unite all our scattered and diverse forces to this vital end?

Chapter 17

Tito and Non-Alignment

When Josip Broz Tito was born in 1892, a superficial observer would have thought that he had entered a very stable and structured world. Empires stretched around the globe, centring on cultured European capitals. Their poverty was concealed, but their opulence was flaunted. Industrialism and imperialism, meshed together, fashioned a universal web of communications. Rebellion must have seemed a distant and hazy memory. The Paris Commune was forgotten by all but a handful of dreamers. In Britain, Queen Victoria's office even asked one of these, the revolutionary poet William Morris, whether he would like to be poet laureate. He would not. The German Social Democrats had newly adopted the Erfurt programme, which was explicitly Marxist; but already critics were accusing them of bureaucracy and dull conformity. Everywhere, as the young Tito arrived, the old order must have seemed safe.

Now the loss of Tito will be lamented by everyone who has followed his work. His contribution to the development of democratic socialism is evident to innumerable students of the Yugoslav system of participation, self-management and socialism. The same William Morris, who disappointed Queen Victoria's Court in the year of Tito's birth, provided the Workers' Control Movement in modern Britain with its watchword: "no man is good enough to be another man's master". In the closing years of the nineteenth century, he wrote a prophetic essay on 'A factory as it might be'. Nowhere in the world has his dream of a free fraternity of producers yet been fully realised. But if Morris were to return to the modern world, who can doubt that he would begin his search for clues to the co-operative commonwealth here in Yugoslavia? Yet it is equally important also to register the decisive importance of another seminal concept of Yugoslavia's founder, that of non-alignment. This is crucial to the future of the world, if indeed the world is to be allowed to have a future.

In 1980, when President Tito died, the old imperial stability had vanished, and the world was in unconcealed turmoil where nothing either old or new seemed safe. Empires had collapsed, but exploitation still condemned vast populations to under-development and worse. East/West rivalry had frozen into a yet colder war, in which re-armament became ever more frenzied and uncontrolled, while the deployment of nuclear weapons was widespread and becoming wider. Slump and mass unemployment had returned to the capitalist world, and stern repression was becoming more common in every zone, including both major power blocs. At a time when many peoples were balanced on the edge of famine, world military spending passed a figure of $1.3 billion a day. The authorities who monitor these matters report that it will pass the figure of $1.6 billion per day rather early in the decade we have just entered. Rightly, the non-nuclear States are uniting to express their strong resentment of the fact that vertical proliferation of nuclear weapons between the superpowers seems to know no rational limits. Indeed, new policies initiated by NATO positively insist on horizontal pro-liferation, with the stationing of so-called 'theatre' weapons in countries which have hitherto been able to eschew the presence of nuclear warheads in their territories.

A deepening slump intensifies these insane pressures, as if it were determined to prove the conventional socialist critique of capitalism to be precisely true. While some economies are ex-periencing a net contraction, military budgets mount consistent-ly. This then means quite literally a policy of guns before butter, or in the modern idiom, nuclear missiles before education, health and welfare. Tito's major statement to the League of Communists of Yugoslavia at their 11th Congress in 1978 gave a characteristically far-sighted and strong warning about the dangers of this renewed arms race.

If every nation had pursued similar policies to those which have been followed by Yugoslavia, then this fateful indictment would not be possible. In the given situation, however, it is en-tirely apposite.

Another statesman, Olof Palme, speaking at the Helsinki Conference of the Socialist International, has drawn attention to the special peril which Europe faces because it has in the main, so far rejected the course of non-alignment. "Europe", he said, "is no special zone where peace can be taken for granted. In actual fact, it is at the centre of the arms race. Granted, the general assumption seems to be that any potential military conflict between the superpowers is going to start some place other than in Europe. But even if that were to be the case, we would have to count on one or the other party — in an effort to gain supremacy — trying to open a front on our continent, as well. As Alva Myrdal has recently pointed out, a war can simply be transported here, even though actual causes for war do not exist. Here there is a ready theatre of war. Here there have been great military forces for a long time. Here there are programmed weapons all ready for action . . ."

Basing himself on this recognition, Palme recalled various earlier attempts to create, in North and Central Europe, nuclear-free zones, from which, by agreement, all warheads were to be excluded.

"Today more than ever there is, in my opinion, every reason to go on working for a nuclear-free zone. *The ultimate objective of these efforts should be a nuclear-free Europe.*" (My emphasis).

Olof Palme's proposal would not be easy to achieve, and no-one has more reason to know this than the small, but crucially significant group of European neutral States. Foremost in experience of the struggle for independence and freedom of action is socialist Yugoslavia, as Tito reported in his address on the sixtieth anniversary of the Communist Movement in Yugoslavia. Pointing up the many difficulties which beset a policy of genuine non-alignment, he said:

"In a world divided into blocs, in which social, economic and political contradictions are still resolved by means of force and outside interference, it has been no easy matter to conduct such a policy, nor is it so today either. We have continually been subjected to various pressures and attempts to make us bow to the policies which are against the interests of our country and our movement. We have been and still are deeply convinced that the bloc politics can resolve none of the essential problems of the world, nor can it open up the prospect of democratisation of international relations for which non-aligned countries are striving. The policy of non-alignment, of which we were one of the co-sponsors, is therefore our permanent policy".

Affirming the results of this prolonged struggle, Tito told the 6th Conference of Heads of State of the Non-Aligned Countries in Havana:

"The results of our activities so far represent a rich harvest.

During the past two decades we have asserted the original principles and objectives of non-alignment as permanent values.

We have resolutely fought for peace, security and freedom in the world.

We have made a substantial contribution to the successful pursuit and outcome of the anti-colonial revolution.

We have codified the principles of active and peaceful co-existence and staunchly advocated their implementation.

We have opposed power politics and foreign interference in all the forms in which they manifest themselves.

We have initiated long-term actions for the establishment of the new international economic order.

We have contributed to the realisation of the universality of the United Nations and to the strengthening of its role and importance.

We have taken marked steps to initiate the solution of the disarmament problem.

We have started a resolute struggle for decolonisation in the field of technology, information, and culture in general."

It is plain, to everyone who cares to look, that this balance sheet is valid. In the field of disarmament in particular, all the most insistent pressures come from nations grouped within the non-aligned movement. The campaign of the Organisation of African Unity for an African Nuclear-free Zone, or the similar campaigns in the Pacific and South Asian areas, are cases in point. Indeed, the only existing Treaty which forbids nuclear warheads over a wide populous area is the Treaty of Tlatelolco, which covers the Latin American continent. Most recently, the rebellion of the non-aligned world at the Geneva Conference which met to review the Non-Proliferation Treaty, and which was rightly unable to agree upon any 'certificate of good health' within this area, constitutes a powerful signal to all in the nuclear-armed States who have eyes to see.

Europe, having generated two world wars, and constituting the prime target for self-destruction in the third, is the slowest of the continents to awaken to these challenges. True, half aware of the menace so properly reported by Palme, Europe has seeded a very large number of partial plans for restricted nuclear-free zones. Central Europe, Baltic, Balkan and Mediterranean free zones have been propounded by numerous statesmen and scholars. But real progress is slow, whilst the arms race is anything but slow.

Now we face in Europe the forced development of the concept of 'theatre' nuclear war, and the rapid emplacement of the military hardware which is making it real.

The conventional notion of nuclear deterrence had always

been wrapped in swathes of assurances by its proponents that the actual use of nuclear weapons was unthinkable. This had been apparently borne out during the Cuba crisis, when, as one American commentator put it, "we were eyeball to eyeball with the Russians, and they blinked". But in today's world, nuclear forces in the superpowers are at near parity, so that nowadays *Time* magazine offers up the pious hope that, next time, both parties might blink at once. Meantime, so vast are the investments tied into the manufacture of nuclear warheads and their delivery systems, that in any real war, it is not their use but their non-use which has become 'unthinkable'. Since we must still presume that neither major power really wishes to destroy the world, we may begin to understand why more and more weight has therefore been placed on this notion of 'theatre' weapons, which it is canvassed, might be actually employed without annihilating the whole of civilisation.

Thus, an unlooked for transformation has come over the logic of deterrence. It followed the development of highly accurate, adaptable and lethal weapons delivery systems. Now this threatens the very survival of European civilisation. In his last speech, to the Stockholm International Peace Research Institute, the Earl Mountbatten, a former Chief of Staff in Britain, and one-time chairman of NATO's military committee, seized the heart of the question:

> "It was not long, however, before smaller nuclear weapons of various designs were produced and deployed for use in what was assumed to be a tactical or theatre war. The belief was that were hostilities ever to break out in Western Europe, such weapons could be used in field warfare without triggering an all-out nuclear exchange leading to the final holocaust.
> *I have never found this idea credible* (my italics). I have never been able to accept the reasons for the belief that any class of nuclear weapons can be categorised in terms of their tactical or strategic purposes."

Another qualified specialist from Britain is Lord Zuckerman, once Chief Scientific Policy Advisor to the British Government. He points at Mountbatten's insistence, saying that he sees no military reality in what is now referred to as tactical or theatre warfare, because in Europe there are no vast deserts or open plains: on the contrary, urban sprawl makes it certain that even accurate strikes at military targets will inevitably destroy huge civilian populations. "I do not believe", Zuckerman told a Pugwash symposium in Canada, "that nuclear weapons could be used in what is now fashionably called a 'theatre war'. I do not believe that any scenario exists which suggests that nuclear weapons could be used in field warfare between two nuclear States without escalation resulting. I know of several such exercises. They all lead to the opposite conclusion. There is no Marquess of Queensbury who would be holding the ring in a nuclear conflict. I cannot see teams of physicists attached to military staffs who would run to the scene of a nuclear explosion and then back to tell their local commanders that the radiation intensity of a nuclear strike by the other side was such and such, and that therefore the riposte should be only a weapon of equivalent yield. If the zone of lethal or wounding neutron radiation of a so-called neutron bomb would have, say, a radius of half a kilometer, the reply might well be a 'dirty' bomb with the same zone of radiation, but with a much wider area of devastation due to blast and fire."

It is often claimed that 'It is not where nuclear weapons come from that matters, it is where they land'. To that we must add that it does not matter, when they land, whether some occult philosopher of war has originally styled them 'tactical' or 'strategic', 'theatre' or otherwise. Once we have seen the trend involved in reasoning about theatre war we cannot fail to draw some very unpleasant conclusions about it.

First, if Mountbatten and Zuckerman are right, any 'theatre' in which such weapons of whatever provenance are used, will be eliminated. Second, the corollary is that if there is any meaning in the restriction implied in the concept of 'theatre' weapons, it is not that they will be selective within a particular zone, but that they might possibly be unleashed in one comparatively narrow area rather than another wider one. That is to say, and this is the whole point, they might be exchanged in Europe prior to 'escalation', which in this case would mean extending their exchange to the USA and the USSR. This carniverous prospect is not at all identical with the simple supposition with which supporters of nuclear disarmament are often (wrongly) credited, that 'one day deterrence will not work'. It rather implies that there has been a mutation in the concept of deterrence itself, with grisly consequences for all of us in Europe.

If the great powers drift into a conflict which requires a bit of a nuclear war, they will want to have it away from home.

If Europeans do not wish to be their hosts for such a match, then, regardless of whether it is right or wrong to suppose that it may be confined to our 'theatre', we must discover a new initiative which can move us towards disarmament. New technologies will not do this, and nor will either superpower find it easy to respond unless there is a significant and powerful pressure upon all concerned so to do.

This involves the search for a political step which can open up new forms of public pressure, and bring into the field of force new moral resources. Partly this is a matter of ending superpower domination of the most important negotiations.

But another part of the response involves a multi-national mobilisation of public opinion. In Europe, this will not materialise until people appreciate the exceptional vulnerability of their continent. Then they will begin to organise for the removal of nuclear weapons from all European soil, East and West alike, and for a new approach to de-alignment. It seems very plain that the gradual and peaceful dismantling of the European blocs can never begin by agreement, until nuclear polarization and escalation is reversed. The goal of a nuclear-free Europe, from the Soviet border to the Portuguese coastline, is beginning to attract serious and thoughtful consideration in many countries. If it can become a campaigning issue, then a whole variety of intermediate steps to ultimate European non-alignment become first conceivable, then practical. Once this progress begins, detente and disarmament may indeed become irreversible processes.

It is for this reason that Tito's testament is burningly relevant far beyond the Yugoslav frontiers, and particularly in a Europe over which the final holocaust may be unleashed at any time. Homage to the memory of a far-sighted man thus reinforces a resolve to carry forward his struggle. Unlike many powerful national leaders, Josip Broz Tito's posthumous influence will increase and widen, as the meaning of the concept of non-alignment comes home, in its full force, to the peoples of our continent.

Chapter 18

Defeat is Indivisible

As the detente collapses around us, sane voices can still be heard. "What can one say" asked the Pope in his New Year message, "in the face of gigantic and threatening military arsenals which especially at the close of 1979 have caught the attention of the World and especially of Europe, both East and West?". What can be said was indeed said, and wisely, by Lord Zuckerman, in a most important article in *The Times* (21 January 1980): "if the battle is for the hearts and souls of men, there is no point in 'winning' one for the hearts of the dead". As chief scientific advisor to the Government from 1964 until 1971, Zuckerman has reason to know what impediments stand in the way of Governmental learning. Yet he insists that "there is no technical road to victory in the nuclear arms race. Defeat is indivisible in a war of nuclear weapons". The Pope, in his address, gave out an awesome list of statistics to confirm this view.

Yet the dangers which already mark the decade we are entering are by no means restricted to the peril arising from the confrontation between the superpowers. In the past these states shared a common, if tenuous interest in the restriction of nuclear military capacity to a handful of countries. Once they were agreed upon a non-proliferation treaty they were able to lean upon many lesser powers to accept it. The USA, the USSR and Britain tested their first successful atomic bombs in 1945, 1949 and 1952. France joined the 'club' in 1960, China in 1964 and India in 1974, when she announced a "peaceful explosion". After a spectacular theft of plans from the Urenco plant in Holland, a peaceful explosion is now expected in Pakistan. Peaceful explosions in South Africa, Israel, Libya, Iraq, Brazil: all are possible, and some may be imminent. One by-product of the Soviet invasion of Afghanistan is the resumption of the supply of American weapons to Pakistan (so much for President Carter's campaign for "human rights") in spite of the clear presumptions involved in the agreement on non-proliferation.

And there is worse news. The announcement of a major programme of development of nuclear power stations in Britain, at a cost which some commentators have assessed as twenty or more billion pounds, does not entail simply a headache for English environmentalists. It seems at least thinkable, indeed plausibly thinkable, that some entrepreneurs have seen the possibility of launching a new boom, supported on technological innovation, following from the random exportation of nuclear power-plants to the Third World. With such plants and a meccano set, together if necessary with some modest bribery or theft, by the end of the 'eighties there may be a Nigerian bomb, an Indonesian bomb, not a proliferation but a plague of deterrents.

Solemnly, we must ask ourselves the question, knowing what we know of the acute social and economic privations which beset vast regions of the world: is it even remotely likely that humanity can live through the next 10 years without experiencing somewhere, between these or the other conflicting parties, an exchange of nuclear warheads? The moral authority of the superpowers in the rest of the world has never been lower. Imperatives of national independence drive more and more peoples to accept that their military survival requires a nuclear component. Even if Afghanistan had never been invaded, even if NATO had not resolved to deploy its new generation of missiles, this burgeoning of destructive power would remain fearful. As things are, the superpowers intensify the terror to unimagined levels.

In this new world of horror, remedies based on national protest movements can never take practical effect, while governments remain locked into the cells of their own strategic assumptions. Yet something *must* be done, if only to arrest the growing possibility of holocaust by accident. After the Soviet troops moved into Kabul, the Communist Party of Italy called upon European Governments to try to resume a mediatory role. Some might like to do this, and others could be pushed. But how can we make sure they *are* pushed?

Perhaps the answer is a new mass campaign, of petitions, marches, meetings, lobbies, for a nuclear-free zone of Europe, stretching from Poland to the Portuguese coastline. All over Europe, the nations should agree that none would house nuclear warheads of any kind.

I do not suggest that such a campaign as this could win easily. But where better than Europe, the most vulnerable of all the continents to the calamities of nuclear war, to begin an act of renunciation which could reverse this unthinkable trend to annihilation?

Afterword

This series of articles came to an end at the beginning of the decade because the birth of the European Nuclear Disarmament campaign set us all quite new tasks.

With the rebirth of the European peace movement, many of the issues which are discussed in this little book begin to present themselves in a new light, with new urgency. Fortunately, new resources are being generated to help to meet them.

At the same time, the rise of Solidarnosc in Poland and its violent repression by a military coup d'etat has continued the 12 year cycle of rebellion and unrest in Eastern Europe. It has also underlined the lessons we have been trying to draw about the threats which are posed to all of us by the continued schism in our continent.

There is more, far more, to be said about all this. But there are more and more of us to say it.